"You need to be tested for your baby's sake," Pete said.

Meredith shook her head, not ready to absorb what he was saying. Every action and reaction in the past seven months had been to protect her child.

Now a stranger on a street corner tells her about a woman to whom she may be related having a disease that could affect the precious life growing within her.

Her husband had been murdered. The men who killed him were after her, and some guy wants to compound the situation?

She couldn't carry any more weight around on her shoulders.

Books by Debby Giusti

Love Inspired Suspense

Nowhere to Hide
Scared to Death
MIA: Missing in Atlanta
*Countdown to Death
*Protecting Her Child

*Magnolia Medical

DEBBY GIUSTI

is a medical technologist who loves working with test tubes and petri dishes almost as much as she loves to write. Growing up as an army brat, Debby met and married her husband—then a captain in the army—at Fort Knox, Kentucky. Together they traveled the world, raised three wonderful army brats of their own and have now settled in Atlanta, Georgia, where Debby spins tales of suspense that touch the heart and soul.

Contact Debby through her Web site, www.DebbyGiusti.com, e-mail debby@debbygiusti.com or write c/o Steeple Hill Books, 233 Broadway, Suite 1001, New York, NY 10279.

Protecting Her Child

Debby Giusti

Steeple Hill®

Published by Steeple Hill Books™

STEEPLE HILL BOOKS

Steeple
Hill®

Recycling programs
for this product may
not exist in your area.

ISBN-13: 978-0-373-44339-0
ISBN-10:   0-373-44339-0

PROTECTING HER CHILD

Before I formed you in the womb I knew you,
before you were born I set you apart; I appointed
you as a prophet to the nations.

—*Jeremiah* 1:5

This book is dedicated to my dear friend,
Pat Rosenbach, who first told me about VHL,
and to her friend, Eva, who had
Von Hippel-Lindau disease.

Although fiction, I hope the story has captured the
courage and determination of all who battle VHL.

ONE

Meredith Lassiter's throat ran dry and her pulse raced as the wind outside whistled through the tall pine trees. The old house moaned in protest, its creaks sounding like footsteps in the night. Ever so slowly, she eased back the edge of the curtain and peered into the darkness.

The steel-gray pickup truck sat like a vulture at the end of the desolate beach road. Tinted windows in the extended cab and covered camper obscured her view of the thugs she knew were hunkered down inside.

Men whose intimidation had forced her to flee her home six months ago and hide in this rental unit where no one asked questions about a woman on the run. Depraved, amoral men who had killed her husband and who now planned to kill her.

Meredith glanced at the table where sections of

the *Georgia Coastal News* lay scattered. Even in the darkened house, she could read the headline. *Suspect Arrested in Payroll Loan Scam.* Two additional men sought for questioning. The article mentioned a possible connection with her husband's murder.

Why had the overzealous reporter added Meredith's name in the same paragraph with the un-identified police informant who had recently come forward?

Be not afraid. The verse from scripture had comforted Meredith in the past. Tonight, the words did little to calm her pulse or the pinpricks of anxiety that scurried along her spine.

The door of the truck swung open, and a man stepped onto the sandy road. He spoke to someone inside the vehicle before he pointed to the tiny cottage that had been her latest refuge.

Her heart crashed against her chest.

Run!

Meredith stumbled into the bedroom and snatched the overnight tote from the closet, a bag she'd packed in case this night ever arrived.

Adrenaline and fear pushed her forward. She reached for her purse and threw the strap over her shoulder. Three steps to the kitchen, and she was at the door. Her hand touched the knob.

She paused for half a second, then raced back to where the baby quilt lay on the couch. Grabbing the fabric she'd patiently stitched over the last few months, she retraced her steps and unlatched the back door.

Meredith peered into the darkness of the backyard. Seeing no one, she slipped into the night.

Pete Worth adjusted the ocular on the microscope until the leukocytes and neutrophils swarmed into view. Eve Townsend's blood smear confirmed that the woman's condition had deteriorated since her last lab appointment at Magnolia Medical.

Exactly as Pete had expected. Being right didn't prevent the sadness that slipped like a dark pall over his shoulders.

He steeled himself to the reality VHL patients eventually had to face. Von Hippel-Lindau disease. Seemed the more bizarre the name, the more convoluted the illness. Just like the twisted tumors that grew within Eve's body.

He hated VHL as much as he was intrigued by the secrets it held. If scientists could understand how to block the blood flow to the tangled cluster of capillaries that formed the tumors, they'd understand how to retard the growth of other malignancies as well.

In time. Pete sighed. Something Eve didn't have.

He glanced up as Denise Ryan, Magnolia Medical's secretary, entered the lab and headed for his workstation. Denise had a big heart as well as an insatiable interest in the personal lives of the technologists on staff.

"Eve's in the waiting room," Denise announced as she neared. "She has a four o'clock appointment with Dr. Davis and wants to hand carry her lab results to his office."

"I thought she was Dr. Fleming's patient."

"She was. But the VHL Institute encouraged her to switch physicians on Sheila Hudson's recommendation. Remember, Sheila drove her son over from Savannah to be treated by Davis."

Pete raised his brow. "Brice died eight months ago, blind and riddled with tumors. That's hardly a favorable recommendation."

Denise sighed. "A tragedy for sure. Still, if I were Eve, I'd try anything or any physician who offered hope. Which is probably why she made the switch. Besides, she told me Davis was a close friend of her parents. Since their deaths, she's stayed in touch."

Davis's treatment protocol was costly and questionable. Pete hated hearing that Eve had succumbed to the hype. She needed hope, but not false hope.

"Tell her I'll send the results to his office electronically."

Denise's eyes softened. She touched his arm. "You know Eve's here to see you."

Pete glanced back at the blood smear. Cells didn't make comments he chose to ignore.

"Eve considers you the son she never had," Denise continued, oblivious to the emotions that swept through Pete, his eyes trained on the array of cells. "If you weren't so fiercely independent and focused on making your own way, you'd accept her love."

"And her money?"

"That's something your father would have said."

She was right, but then, Denise had known his dad.

Despite working for Eve's parents and living in the caretaker's lodge on their vast estate, Pete's father had been bitterly vocal about his disregard for the wealthy Townsend family. A by-product of the jealousy he felt after Pete's mother's untimely death, no doubt.

"I've got her lab slips." Pete pointed to the printouts, lying next to the microscope. "Tell Eve I'll be out after I finish her CBC."

As Denise left the lab, Pete turned his attention to Eve's test results. Chemistry profile, urinalysis, CBC.

An unexpected and unwelcome lump filled his throat. Clinical lab tests didn't lie. One kidney surgically removed two years ago. Renal cell carcinoma in the remaining organ. Dialysis might help initially, but the eventual prognosis was kidney failure and death.

Grabbing the slips off the counter, Pete squared his shoulders and walked purposefully toward the waiting room. His resolve melted when he caught sight of Eve.

Fragile. Frail.

His gut tightened. This was the part of medicine he didn't like.

She sat on the edge of the straight-back chair, her arms draped with one of the quilted stoles she stitched to occupy her fingers while the disease ate through her body.

Forty-two on her next birthday, she was meticulously groomed in silk pants and a matching jacket. Her hair and tasteful makeup accentuated her green eyes and high cheekbones, camouflaging the sallow skin and pale complexion hidden underneath.

Critically ill, she looked older than her years, yet her smile when she glanced up and saw Pete was anything but melancholy. For half a heartbeat, he longed to go back in time to when he was a little boy wrapped in her embrace.

Clearing his throat, he forced the thought to flee and held out the lab slips. "Denise said you're seeing Dr. Davis today."

Eve raised her brow as she took the forms. "From your tone of voice, I take it you don't think I should have changed physicians?"

"You don't need my approval, Eve."

"But I value your opinion."

"Evidently you value Sheila's more."

Her face clouded momentarily, making him regret his hasty retort.

"Sheila founded the Institute as a source of information for VHL patients and their families. I trust her judgment, Pete."

"Of course you do." He softened. This wasn't the time to open old wounds.

When he had started working at Magnolia Medical a few months back, he knew Eve would be one of the patients the outstanding research and clinical lab facility served. What he hadn't expected was the raw emotion he felt each time he saw her.

"Sheila stopped by to see me when she came to Atlanta last week," Eve said.

"How's she doing?"

"Managing to put up a good front. Brice was twenty-one, but she still considered him her baby."

Eve shook her head and tried to smile. "I remember when she told me she was pregnant. It was at your fifth birthday party."

The extravagant event Eve had thrown for him, open to the estate staff and their children. "A celebration your parents weren't happy about when they returned from Europe," he reminded her.

"My parents didn't approve of a lot of things I did."

"Like befriending the caretaker's kid?"

"You needed love, Pete, and I needed a child to dote on. Seems we were good for each other in spite of what they thought."

"Bucking authority is never easy. I owe you my thanks."

"You don't owe me anything. You know that. Although I wish you'd let me help. At least with funding for your research."

He held up his hand, palm out. "Eve, please. We've had this conversation before."

Her purse sat on the floor. In an obvious attempt to change the subject, she bent and searched the contents before pulling out a photograph. "I told you I wanted to find my daughter. The private investigator I hired located her."

Eve had always been forthright about her past. Unmarried and pregnant at seventeen, her only recourse—or so her parents had insisted—was to put the baby up for adoption. Struggling with the pain of giving up her child, Eve had found comfort in the Lord.

A testament to His healing grace, she often claimed.

Not that Pete fell for the religious hype. Eve could keep her God. He would depend on his own abilities to get through tough times.

She held up the photo. A bleached blonde with widespread eyes, flat nose and an underdeveloped upper lip.

Pete stared at the picture. "I thought the lawyer who handled the adoption died years ago."

"That's right. But the P.I. located the records. The Collins family, who adopted my baby, lived in Augusta at that time. They named her Dixie. She currently lives in Craddock Sound."

"About eighty miles south of Fort Stewart."

"You know the area?"

"I spent three years at Fort Stewart with the army after my tour in the Middle East."

Eve averted her eyes. Absent during that portion of his life, she didn't comment, but returned instead to the subject at hand.

"Sam and Hazel Collins received their baby girl on November sixteenth, the day I delivered. Dixie's driver's license and social security card verify she's who she says she is." Eve pointed to the woman in the photo. "I'm sure Dixie Collins is my daughter."

Who doesn't look a thing like you, Pete wanted to add. Besides, there was something unsettling about the blonde.

The photo's resolution wasn't the best, still…?

He had never known Eve to touch alcohol, yet the woman who claimed to be Eve's daughter had the facial characteristics of a person born to a mother who drank excessively. Fetal alcohol syndrome.

Not that he'd mention it to Eve. Not now. Not until he learned more about the unlikely daughter. A phony driver's license and social security card were easy enough to come by. The vast fortune Eve's rightful heir stood to inherit could make a number of people claim to be the missing daughter.

"Of course, my attorneys insist on DNA testing to confirm that she's my daughter."

Thank goodness for lawyers.

Eve glanced at her watch, then back at Pete. "I need to head to Dr. Davis's office before the after-noon traffic."

For a moment, she searched his face as if she, too, were remembering the past. Then she adjusted the stole around her shoulders, grabbed her purse and stood.

"You lived on the estate for twelve years, Pete. It's still your home. Don't be a stranger."

Flashing a smile that touched the depths of his soul, she walked away, her heels clicking against the polished tile floor.

A chunk of his defensive armor began to crumble. He pulled in a fortifying breath. Eve and her parents had turned their backs on him years ago. Despite their actions, he wanted to help Eve and people who suffered the way she did, but relating to cells in a petri dish was different to dealing with someone face-to-face. Bottom line, he wouldn't open himself to rejection again.

A door slammed. Magnolia Medical's research department manager walked toward him, a file folder in her left hand.

"I had a call from Jamal Washington." Veronica Edwards's smile grew as she approached. "He wanted to brag about his favorite graduate student. Your use of antiangiogenic drugs to stop blood flow to VHL tumors is impressive, Pete."

His cheeks burned. As much as he appreciated Veronica's praise, he needed help with his funding more than adulation.

"I took your request to the board. Magnolia Medical can provide some assistance." She opened the folder and handed him a form with a five-digit figure highlighted in the top paragraph. "A start, although I know it's not enough to cover all your research. No doubt, the VHL Institute will provide additional support."

"I'm not applying for their grant."

"Eve isn't the Institute's only contributor. There are others."

"Whose donations pale in comparison. I won't accept her help."

"Look, Pete, I don't know the whole story. Denise mentioned something about your father. But whatever happened was a long time ago."

"Please, Veronica."

She held up her hand. "Just don't let your pride get in the way of saving lives. Applications for the Institute grant are due Tuesday. At least think it over. I'm giving you Monday off so you can use the long weekend to weigh your options."

Without waiting for his response, Veronica turned back to the lab, leaving Pete to stare out the large windows that overlooked the parking lot.

His eyes focused on Eve scurrying toward her car. Her shoulders slumped forward ever so slightly, as if the effort of walking was almost more than her sickly body could manage.

Heaviness filled Pete's heart. His father had cared more about the estate grounds than he had for the little boy who yearned to be loved. Eve had been Pete's refuge. She'd showered him with affection. As a child, he'd responded in kind.

Love, connection, a sense of family was what they both had needed then and, if the truth were known, probably needed now.

Although Pete never told Eve, he'd gone into medical research because of her, hoping to find a cure for the disease that would eventually take her life. But he couldn't change Eve's lab results, and no matter how quickly his research proceeded, he wouldn't find answers that would help her in time. Yet he could ensure that she didn't give her heart and her fortune to someone who didn't legally have a claim to either.

Craddock Sound? He had three days. Enough time to do a little reconnaissance. Hopefully, Pete would find out the truth about Eve's supposed daughter.

TWO

Pete downed the last drops of the thirty-two-ounce cola he'd bought at the gas station as he turned off the highway and glanced at his BlackBerry sitting on the console. Thank goodness for mobile technology and the fact that Dixie Collins's phone number had been listed in the phone book, along with her address. MapQuest provided the missing link.

For the last two hours, Pete had sat parked down a lonely stretch of back road in sight of Dixie's modest home. Hurry up and wait. Just like in the army.

From the number of times she had stepped outside to use her cell phone, Pete wondered if something were going down.

He needed patience. And another cola.

His watch read 11:45 p.m. Time for Dixie to get some shut-eye.

Pete wouldn't mind catching a few winks himself.

He pushed the seat back to its full extension and stretched his legs. Rubbing a hand over his eyes, he was just about to nod off when he heard an engine. Startled, he straightened.

A Lincoln Town Car pulled into the driveway. Green body, white vinyl top, mid-nineties vintage.

The driver stepped onto the pavement. Six-two, if not a tad taller, and at least 250 pounds of muscle. He wore his hair pulled back in a ponytail at the base of his neck and was dressed in a dark T-shirt and jeans.

Dixie ran to greet him. Wrapping her arms around his neck, the two embraced and shared a lingering kiss.

Follow your gut, Pete's first sergeant used to remind him. Right now, his gut was screaming that something wasn't on the up-and-up about this late-night rendezvous.

Once the loving couple unwound, they climbed into the Lincoln and headed out along the two-lane road.

Pete gave them enough leeway to keep from attracting attention before he followed the taillights that cut through the night.

Staying clear of the main highway, Dixie and

her boyfriend headed north, meandering along the coastal contours. Eventually, the two-lane road veered east into a narrow spit of black desolation.

If they'd made Pete, the lonely road could be a trap. But Pete felt no sense of unease or warning.

The taillights turned, and Pete increased his speed. He couldn't lose them now.

An outline of homes sat nestled along a coastal inlet. A plaque erected on the side of the road welcomed him to Refuge Bay.

Driving on the main thoroughfare of the small community, Pete passed two gas stations, both closed, a corner mom-and-pop grocery and an all-night diner, where three patrons sat at a booth by the window.

On the far side of town, a long, shingled building was perched at the edge of the water. A sign out front read REFUGE LODGE.

At the next intersection, the Lincoln turned inland. Were they going in a circle? Or had he been spotted?

The boyfriend didn't look like the type of guy who enjoyed being followed. Hopefully, this cat-and-mouse game they'd been playing wouldn't end up with Pete in the trap.

Not a good thought.

As if in response, the Lincoln stopped short by a tiny bungalow.

Pete cut his lights and turned onto a path that led behind a clump of pines. He killed the engine, crawled out of his Jeep and watched the guy push open the rear door of the small frame house. Dixie followed him inside. Lights flipped on from room to room.

Hoping to catch a glimpse of what was happening, Pete circled to the far side of the wooden structure and wormed his way through the thick shrubbery until he could peer in the window.

The man stood over a small table, his face twisted into a deep frown. A newspaper lay open. He shoved it aside, then lifted a square of cloth and studied it for a moment before tucking it into his pocket. Evidently satisfied with what he found, he turned abruptly, motioned to Dixie and headed for the door.

If Pete left the cover of the bushes now, he'd be spotted. Better to hole up until they climbed into the car and started down the road. With a little luck, Pete would be able to backtrack and pick up their tail.

Hunkered down in the bushes, Pete listened for the sound of an engine. All he heard were tree frogs against the backdrop of the distant surf.

Two doors slammed and an engine purred into gear.

Pete climbed from the bramble as the Lincoln drove out of sight, probably heading back to Dixie's house. He glanced at the bungalow. Torn between seeing what had prompted the twosome to drive so far in the middle of the night and wanting to follow them, he crossed the road and stepped into a small kitchen. Neat. Clean. A bowl of fruit sat on the counter. An open pantry next to the back door held a few cans of vegetables, a box of oatmeal and a jar of pickles.

The design on the linoleum was old and faded but without a spot or crumb. The floorboards creaked as he walked into the living–dining room combination where a love seat and rocker edged a braided rug. A wooden crate, decorated with a collection of seashells, served as a coffee table. Two folding chairs and a card table sat in the dining area.

Swatches of fabric that had drawn the guy's interest lay on the table in various pastel patterns of tiny, delicate hearts and crosses. Pete drew closer, overwhelmed by a sense of familiarity. The intricate motif looked like something Eve would create.

Glancing into the bedroom, he smelled a fresh, floral fragrance as sweet as honeysuckle. Had to be a woman's room.

Blow-up mattress on the floor. Rumpled bedding, the beige blanket and pink top sheet thrown aside.

Had someone or something interrupted her sleep? Not Dixie and her friend. The house hadn't been occupied when they had entered through the back door.

A photo on the floor next to the bed caught Pete's attention. A woman with shoulder-length raven hair and green eyes the color of the ocean looked lovingly at a man, perhaps two inches taller, who held her close.

For an instant, Pete longed for something as real in his life.

Abruptly, he turned away. Whoever lived here didn't need her privacy violated.

Stepping into the kitchen, he spied a stack of bills on the counter addressed to Meredith Lassiter. Probably the gal in the photo.

He glanced at the open pantry, noting the black hinges attached to the doorframe.

Odd.

He retraced his steps to the bedroom.

A couple of pairs of slacks and a blouse hung on the rack in the closet. Slippers were neatly placed on the floor below.

He hadn't noticed earlier, but the closet door had been removed from its hinges, just like the pantry.

Some type of space-saving decorating trick?

Then Pete left the house, the lights still ablaze to

warn the woman, should she return before the break of day. Tomorrow he'd make more inquiries in town. Hopefully, he'd learn why Dixie and her friend had driven through the night to break into this bungalow.

A second question needed to be answered as well.

Who was Meredith Lassiter?

"Are you a policeman?"

Not the response Pete expected from the shop-keeper.

"No, ma'am, but I am trying to find Meredith Lassiter." He paused, searching for a way to ease the concern he saw in the woman's eyes. Gray hair, mid-sixties, she continued to stare at him.

"I'm a friend of her mother's." Pete needed the woman's cooperation. "One of Meredith's neighbors said she teaches quilting classes here at your store."

"Taught. Past tense. She's missed her last three classes and hasn't answered her cell in days."

The friend-of-the-mother angle must have worked, although annoyance was still evident in the shopkeeper's voice. Hopefully aimed at Meredith and not at him.

"I left a message, reminding her that she's got a check to pick up," the woman continued. "With the economy and all, I don't have to tell you money's tight."

He thought of the lack of funding for his research. "Yes, ma'am."

The woman shrugged and worried her fingers. The frustration he'd heard earlier in her voice softened to concern. "I thought she'd be back by now. Truth be told, I'm worried about Meredith. She's a delightful young woman with a big heart. I wouldn't want anything to happen to her."

Pulling out his business card, Pete placed it on the counter. "I'm staying at the Lodge over the weekend. If she comes back, would you tell her that Pete Worth is looking for her?"

"Shall I mention her mother?"

"No." Pete glanced at the colorful quilts displayed around the shop. "Her quilting. Tell Meredith I'm interested in her work."

The woman's eyes softened. "She *is* gifted."

"Do you happen to know where I could find her boyfriend?" Pete thought back to the bedroom photo. "The guy's about her age, maybe a few inches taller. Dark hair, long sideburns?"

The shopkeeper furrowed her brow. "Doubt there'd be a boyfriend this soon after her husband's death. I heard the police are calling it a homicide."

A buzz sounded in Pete's ears. Like a trapped fly. His own internal warning system. Seemed the deeper he dug, the more problems surfaced. His desire to help Eve had led him to Dixie and now to a missing woman whose husband may have been murdered.

Getting involved in a homicide investigation wasn't on his list of things to do this weekend, but if Meredith knew Dixie, she might provide information that Eve needed to know.

"Ma'am, do you recall when her husband died?"

"Hmmm? Must have been six months ago or so. Meredith never talked about him, and most folks didn't connect her with the story in the paper. Seems he died on a fishing boat out of Jackson Harbor."

"South of here?"

"That's right. The article said he'd just hired on. Went out on a day trip, and his leg got tied up in one of the nets as it was being tossed in the water. According to the story, he was pulled overboard, and the blades on the motor caught him. Cut him pretty bad. He bled to death before they could get him to shore."

"They?"

"The crew. I wouldn't have thought much more about the accident except the paper ran a picture of the wife he left behind, and Meredith arrived in town not long after that. Last week the police arrested the boat owner."

If the husband had been involved in something criminal, Dixie and her boyfriend could be as well. Perhaps that's why they'd made the late-night visit to Meredith's bungalow.

Pete pointed to the counter where he'd placed his card. "You have my cell number. Be sure to tell Meredith I'm looking for her."

"Do you know that other guy who stopped by? He wouldn't say what he wanted."

Pete thought of Dixie's friend. "Big man with a ponytail?"

The shopkeeper shook her head. "The man was Latino, probably five-eight." She touched her face. "He had a scar on his left cheek."

Evidently, Dixie and her boyfriend weren't the only other people looking for Meredith. The shopkeeper had mentioned the police, who probably wanted a chat with the grieving widow as well.

Leaving the store, Pete headed down the block to the diner and sat in a booth that faced the street with a clear view of the quilt shop. Three cups of coffee later, he noticed an elderly woman shuffle inside, holding a cane in her right hand. One of the few people who had visited the shop that morning.

Pete caught the eye of the waitress and pointed to his cup, which she quickly refilled.

Taking a sip of the hot brew, he glanced once again at the shop. The old woman stepped through the door and onto the sidewalk.

This time she held the cane in her left hand.

A baggy sweater hung over her sweatpants. A floppy hat covered her hair, except for a long strand that trailed along the slender curve of her neck.

The same raven hair he'd seen in the bungalow photo.

Pete threw some bills on the table and raced from the diner.

The woman turned the corner and crossed the street. A clunker sat parked at the end of the block.

Nervously, she glanced over her shoulder. Spying him, she tossed her cane aside and ran toward the car. Her hat flew off, and dark hair spilled across her shoulders, swinging back and forth.

She had an awkward gait and kept her hands close to her body. Was she holding something?

He was gaining on her.

"Meredith, wait," Pete called. "I need to talk to you."

She flicked another glance at him. Fear flashed across her face.

Not what he wanted.

At that moment, a police cruiser turned onto the block.

Meredith stopped abruptly. She turned and caught Pete's eye, her own wide with panic.

He slowed his pace. Meredith paused long enough for the black-and-white sedan to pass before she took off running again.

Silhouetted for that brief moment against the backdrop of the brick building behind her, Pete realized something he hadn't noticed before.

Meredith Lassiter was pregnant.

THREE

After everything that had happened, Meredith's internal radar was set on high. She glanced over her shoulder to ensure that no one new had entered the bank before she counted the money and stepped away from the teller. A month's wages for teaching classes at the quilt shop wouldn't take her far, but at least she had some cash.

Had they found her because she'd used her credit card? She'd tried to be careful, but the prenatal vitamins and the fresh fruits and vegetables she ate to protect her baby's health cost more than red beans and rice. Last week, she'd been forced to charge her groceries. The steel-gray pickup had appeared on her street a few days later.

Coincidence? Maybe, but she wouldn't risk charging anything again. At least until she ran out of money.

What about the guy who had chased after her today? Too many unfamiliar people were appearing in her life. Life-threatening complications that sent her nerve endings into alert mode.

Her immediate need was to get as far from Refuge Bay as possible. Find a safe place to hole up, then a job and an obstetrician.

Thankfully, she'd escaped from the bungalow in time. The last two days spent living out of her car made her overdue for a hot shower and a good meal.

She shoved the bills into her purse, her thoughts once again on the guy she'd seen earlier.

An all-American type with his dark polo shirt, khaki slacks and short hair. Maybe a reporter? She hadn't spilled anything to the police, and she certainly wouldn't divulge information to a stringer looking for a story. Not that she had much to tell.

Peering through the bank's thick glass doors, she glanced up and down the street, searching for a pickup with an extended cab and tinted windows.

Two minivans drove by. Soccer moms with their brood of kids. Nothing to fear.

Meredith swallowed the wad of anxiety that seemed perpetually lodged in her throat, pushed open the door and stepped into the humid outdoors. The briny smell of the sea hung in the early spring air.

Regret filtered past her with the breeze. She'd miss the ocean when she left Refuge Bay, but she wouldn't miss the nervous apprehension that continually bubbled up, causing her chest to burn and her head to pound.

Just as long as the stress didn't affect the baby. *Bless this child, dear Lord. Let nothing harm the precious gift You've given me.*

Purse draped over her shoulder, she rubbed her hand protectively over her belly as she rounded the corner and nearly collided headlong into the guy who had chased her earlier.

She did a hasty about-face, ready to run back to the bank.

He grabbed her arm. Twisting, she tried to break free.

"Ma'am, please. I won't hurt you. I work in an Atlanta medical lab. My name's Pete Worth."

She glanced down at the fingers wrapped around her arm.

He relaxed his grasp and dropped his hand. "Please, don't run away."

Raising her gaze, she noted concern in his dark brown eyes.

"What do you want?" she demanded, keeping her shoulders back, her chin jutting forward. No need to cut him any slack.

He drew a business card from his pocket. "Information about a woman named Dixie Collins."

She took a step back. Collins? "I...I don't know anyone named Dixie."

The lab guy crooked a brow and leaned in closer. He raised a finger to her eye. "You've got a little brown dot in your iris."

The mark she'd had since birth. Her adoptive father called it the devil's curse. Not what a child needed to hear.

"Look, I don't have time for this," she said with a huff.

He held up his hand. "Sam Collins and his wife Hazel adopted a baby twenty-four years ago."

Meredith's world shifted. Vertigo or lack of food, but for half a second, everything swirled around her.

"The infant was born on November sixteenth." He stepped closer. "The Collins family lived in Augusta, Georgia, at the time. Now a woman named Dixie claims she's the adopted daughter."

Questions flew through her mind, not that she'd give them voice.

"I'm helping Eve Townsend, the birth mother, find her rightful heir." He stared at her, waiting for a reply.

Meredith swallowed, trying to form a response.

"Seems…seems to me someone who gave her child up for adoption wouldn't want to revisit the past," she managed to stammer.

"Unless the woman's dying."

His words hit Meredith hard. "Dying?"

Pete looked past her down the street. "Is there someplace we can talk? A coffee shop? Or the diner? I'll buy you lunch."

She shook her head. Much as she wanted to believe the man with the even gaze and the calming voice, she'd learned things weren't always as they seemed.

She took the offered card. "I need to go."

Frustration washed over his face. "Eve has the same mark on the iris of her eye, which you evidently inherited from your biological mother. She also has a fatal genetic condition that could have been passed on as well." He glanced at Meredith's belly. "You need to be tested, for your baby's sake."

She shook her head, not ready to absorb what he was saying. Every action and reaction she'd had in the last seven months had been to protect her child.

Now a stranger she didn't know tells her about a woman to whom she may be related, and a disease that could adversely affect the precious life growing within her.

Her husband had been murdered. The men who'd

killed him were after her, and this guy wanted to compound the situation?

For all she knew, he could be working with the thugs. Right now, she couldn't trust her instincts, and the last thing she needed was another problem to weigh her down.

Meredith took another step back.

"Wait. I didn't mean to scare you," he insisted.

She turned, needing space and time to process everything he'd just thrown her way.

"I'm staying at the Lodge. Think it over and we can meet later."

Meredith dashed around the corner and stumbled into the alleyway on the far side of the bank.

She wasn't ready to trust anyone. Certainly not the police, who hadn't believed her when she was a child and had questioned her more than she felt necessary after her husband's death. Had they thought she was somehow involved?

Her hand brushed over the rough brick wall. She needed support. Her world was in chaos and shifting far too quickly out of control.

Two months before delivery wasn't the time to be thrown off track because of a woman who had a deathbed wish to right a mistake she'd made twenty-four years ago.

Pete had mentioned Atlanta, so Meredith wouldn't

head west. Charleston and Hilton Head were up the coast. Maybe the Carolinas would offer a safe haven.

She found her car and fell into the front seat. For a moment, she stared at the business card.

Who was she kidding? She had no place to go and no one to help her. If things didn't change soon, her child would be born into a life on the run.

She needed to know more about the disease that could affect her baby.

The way she looked at it, she had two options. Hit the road to nowhere or find out what Pete Worth had to say.

Pete sat on the deck and watched the boat dock at the neighboring marina. Gulls cawed overhead as waves lapped against the side of the fishing vessel. The day's catch must have been good the way the birds swooped low over the deck, begging for scraps of fish.

The setting sun cast the sky in shades of pink and blue like a patchwork quilt. Something Eve might create with her tiny stitches and pieced fabric.

Or Meredith.

The brown pigment on her left eye was identical to Eve's. Seems Dixie Collins—whoever she was— had led him to Eve's long-lost daughter.

He doubted that Meredith knew about the vast

wealth that would fall into her lap if she and Eve reconnected. Unless Dixie or the boyfriend had told her.

Although that seemed unlikely, since Dixie was trying to pass herself off as the legitimate heir.

Nice gal, huh? She needed a lesson in honesty and integrity and the worth of a person's word.

The shopkeeper had mentioned a Latino who was looking for Meredith. Could he be in cahoots with Dixie and her boyfriend?

Pete needed more information to take back to Eve. Surely, she wouldn't fall into the trap of believing the blond impostor was her child?

Not if Pete could set her straight.

He glanced at his BlackBerry on the glass tabletop. All afternoon, he'd waited for its insistent chirp, hoping Meredith would call.

After she'd scurried off earlier, he'd driven back to her bungalow in hopes that she might return home. He'd go there again tomorrow, just in case. Hopefully, she wasn't on I-95 heading north…or south.

His last recourse was to talk to the police. Not that he wanted to stir up trouble for Meredith, but Eve needed to know the truth.

The ocean scene soothed his unease. Far out at sea, a trawler moved along the horizon.

His BlackBerry rang, breaking the serenity.

Raising it to his ear, he heard Meredith's voice. "Go south out of Refuge Bay for eight miles and take the left fork in the road. At the third stoplight, turn left again and then right at the water's edge. You'll see the Dock House Restaurant straight ahead. I'll meet you there."

"Meredith—"

The phone disconnected.

Relieved that she'd called, Pete hustled to his car and followed her directions.

He found the modest wooden building, weather-worn and in need of repair. Inside, the place seemed clean and the waitress welcoming. He asked for a booth in the corner with a view of the water and the door.

Pete ordered a cola, which the waitress refilled twice and downed a fish sandwich and fries fast enough to leave his stomach burning with indigestion. An hour later, he paid his bill, left the waitress a sizable tip and headed back to his car, annoyed at being stood up.

As he climbed into his Jeep, he hit the RECEIVED file on his BlackBerry, highlighted the most recent incoming number and punched the green CALL button.

A gravelly male voice answered after the fourth ring. "Lloyd's Laundry."

Meredith hadn't used her own phone to call him with directions to this waterfront eatery. Instead, she'd stopped at a Laundromat and placed the call from there, on a landline, like a woman used to covering her tracks.

"Someone phoned me earlier from this number," Pete explained. "Have you seen a woman with black hair, about five-five?"

"I'm just washing my clothes, buddy. Haven't seen anyone tonight except a pregnant gal when I first arrived. She left about an hour ago."

Of course, she'd moved on. If he were lucky, she'd call again.

And if not?

He'd be back to square one.

Frustrated with his luck—or lack of it—Pete started the ignition and turned onto the road leading back to Refuge Bay.

Meredith's phone call had sent him out of town. For what reason? To give her time to break into his room and rummage through his belongings?

Not that she looked like a con artist, but still…

She was carrying Eve's grandchild. Was that skewing his common sense?

Meredith watched Pete pull his Jeep into the motel parking lot, turn off the ignition and step onto the pavement. Hopefully, he wouldn't see her hiding in the shadows.

He studied the surrounding area of tall pines, then locked his car and headed for his room.

Meredith waited ten minutes. The quiet fishing town folded up by nine o'clock this early in spring. The hum of a car engine would announce someone's arrival along the two-lane road that led to the Lodge. All she heard were waves slapping against the beach.

Cautiously, she edged around the side of the building and picked her way down a path through the sea oats that led to the beach. Once her shoes sank into the soft sand, she stopped and looked back at the motel. A long common deck area and pool stretched in front of the row of rooms. Most sat empty.

A light glowed in Pete's window. She'd left the lamp on, as she'd found it earlier when she'd searched the room, being careful to put everything back in its place. Not that he had brought much with him to Refuge Bay, only a change of clothes and some toilet articles stuck in a zippered case marked with the Magnolia Medical logo.

A phone call to the lab confirmed that he worked there, although the receptionist had declined to provide any additional information, and Meredith hadn't left a message when she'd been connected to his voice mail.

At least she knew that part of his story was true. He worked at Magnolia Medical.

She glanced once again at the weathered facade of the old Lodge. The sliding-glass door that led to the deck was open, and Pete stood in the doorway. Peering at him from the shadows, Meredith wondered why this man had stumbled into her life, especially so close on the heels of her recent middle-of-the-night encounter with the two guys in the pickup.

Was Pete just a nice guy trying to right her birth mother's past wrong? Or was his lab persona a ruse to trick her into letting down her guard?

Her first priority was her baby. She needed the information Pete promised to provide about a disease that could threaten the fragile life growing within her.

With a heavy sigh, Meredith pulled her cell from her purse, tapped in the number from Pete's business card and pushed the green button.

"Meet me on the beach," she said when he answered her call.

God willing, in the next few minutes, she'd find out about the mother she'd never known and the disease they both might carry.

Most important, she would learn if that legacy had been passed on to her child.

FOUR

Pete's heart lurched as Meredith emerged from the darkness. Light from the Lodge spilled over the sand and caught her in its path. The wind tugged at her hair. She raised her hand to pull the wayward strands into some type of order, exposing the heavy ring of sadness that surrounded her like a shroud.

No woman, especially one just a few months short of delivery, should have to carry such a heavy burden, let alone something as palpable as what he saw staring back at him.

He hopped down from the deck, but continued to keep his distance. Hopefully, she wouldn't run. He pointed to a row of wooden beach chairs lined up on the sand. "We'll be able to talk there."

She nodded and followed him. He brushed off one of the seats and motioned for her to sit as he hunkered down on the bench directly opposite.

"I called your lab," she said. "The receptionist confirmed that you work at Magnolia Medical."

"Looks like you rummaged around in my motel room as well. Do you believe me now?"

"I'm willing to listen to what you have to say."

"Fair enough." Pete hoped what he said wouldn't alter the rather tenuous truce they'd just reached. "Your mother's name is Eve Townsend. She's a good woman with a big heart. Evidently, she was rather obstinate as a teen and balked against her restrictive parents. There was a boy, a little older than she was. They were in love." Pete shrugged. "Things happened."

"So I'm the love child she gave away." Meredith's tone of voice hovered between anger and regret.

"At her parents' insistence." Pete thought of the Townsends' strict rules and harsh censure of anything but the most proper behavior. "Eve wanted to keep you, but her parents were unrelenting. They said adoption into a loving family would be better for the baby."

Meredith groaned. Her shoulders slumped ever so slightly. "Loving family? What was the criterion they used?"

Evidently, Sam and Hazel Collins hadn't been the best of parents.

"The Townsends went through a trusted lawyer," Pete continued, hoping to convince Meredith of the wealthy family's good intentions. "He assured them you would be well cared for."

She swallowed hard. "Does she have other children?"

He shook his head. "Eve never married. Shortly after you were born, she started having medical problems. Tumors developed, and she was diagnosed with a disease called Von Hippel-Lindau."

"Tumors? Are they cancerous?"

"Not at the onset, although they do cause problems. They can attack various organs. Sometimes the retina. Or the spinal cord. Often the adrenal gland."

She listened attentively.

"When the disease zeros in on the kidneys, the tumors turn malignant. Researchers are now trying to determine which forms of kidney cancer are related to VHL."

"You're saying some people don't know they have the disease?"

"That's right. VHL can go undetected until a major organ is affected. It's a genetic disease that can be inherited from either parent. Or it can appear sporadically for no known reason."

"And Eve's kidneys are involved?"

"She had one removed two years ago. Renal cell carcinoma was diagnosed a few months back."

With her arms wrapped protectively over the child within her belly, Meredith looked vulnerable, and Pete's heart went out to her. She deserved more than the bad news he'd come bearing.

"Eve wants you to know about VHL so you can be tested. You might not carry the disease."

"But if I do, I could pass VHL on to my baby."

"It's a possibility. Eve can explain everything."

Meredith narrowed her eyes. "I don't want to see her."

Pete hadn't expected the depth of emotion he heard in her response. "Please, Meredith—"

"Do you know what a child thinks when her mother abandons her?" She dropped her gaze and picked at the edge of her sweater. "A child thinks she's unlovable. That she's done something wrong. That she deserves the scolding and lectures. That she deserves to be—"

Her voice hitched, and he saw the angry tears that glistened in her eyes.

She swiped her hand over her face and sniffed. "I've cried enough in my life. I don't want to cry anymore. Tell her thanks for the invitation to reconnect, but I'll pass."

She stood and started to race away.

Pete hurried after her. "At least be tested. I can draw your blood at my laboratory. You don't have to meet your mother."

"I've got your number. I'll think it over."

He grabbed her arm, causing her to turn. Once again, the light from the Lodge played over her face.

"What are you involved in, Meredith?"

"Meaning?"

"Were Dixie Collins and her boyfriend working with you and your husband?"

Her eyes widened. "I don't know what you're talking about."

"Dixie and her boyfriend broke into your house last night."

She flinched. "But how—?"

"I wanted information to take to Eve so I followed them."

Meredith took a step back. "I don't know anything about you, Pete Worth, and you know even less about me. Why don't you climb into your Jeep and head back to Atlanta? You can tell Eve that Dixie's her daughter for all I care. I'll have my baby tested when my life gets a little more stable. But right now, I need some space."

Before he could say anything else, she ran from the beach, kicking the sand with her feet.

If only Pete could convince her to return with him to Atlanta.

He had two more days before he needed to be back at Magnolia Medical. He'd make sure Meredith didn't stray too far in case she changed her mind.

The headlights cut through the darkness. Meredith blinked back hot tears that stung her eyes. She wasn't going to cry.

Driving down this winding coastal road demanded her full attention. She couldn't afford to let down her guard.

VHL. Her baby could be at risk. Why should a tiny unborn infant be saddled with something life-threatening? Not the legacy any child wanted to inherit from its mother.

Anger welled up within her, and she wanted to scream against the injustice. Not her baby.

Didn't she have enough to worry about right now?

What about Dixie Collins? Why would she pretend to be Eve's daughter?

Meredith's only possessions were a small overnight bag, a quilt she'd made for her baby and enough cash in her pocket for a week of food and hopefully as many nights in a low-rent motel. Until she could find another job and earn more money.

Her hand instinctively patted her protruding stomach. Two months and her baby would be born. How could she work then? Perhaps she could do sewing alterations or take on consignments. But piecework wouldn't provide enough income to survive.

Meredith pulled in a leveling breath and touched her pocket, where she'd tucked her husband's pocketknife. The knife he'd forgotten to take the day he'd been killed.

Right now, the weight of the weapon provided reassurance. She needed to be careful, yes. But not paranoid.

No one had followed her out of Refuge Bay. She hadn't seen another car along the coastal road for miles. No steel-gray pickup truck. No ruffians who thought they could push her around. No one who knew she was on the run.

She rested her shoulders against the back of the seat, feeling her taut muscles relax ever so slightly. The baby kicked and she almost laughed.

"Hey there, little one. I know I'm not alone. You and I are in this together. And with the help of God, we'll make it."

The roadway straightened into a long stretch of two-lane road. She checked her speed. Fatigue weighed heavily on her. She needed sleep. And not in the front seat of the car.

She longed to stretch out her legs and prop her head on a feathery pillow. Eight hours of uninterrupted slumber would brighten her outlook and ease the dull ache that twisted up her spine.

She cracked open the window, allowing the cool night air to circulate through the car. Readjusting the backrest, she shook her head, hoping to be free of the lethargy that had her in its grip, and reached for the radio knob. Before her fingers pushed the button, she caught a flash of light in the rearview mirror.

Meredith pulled her hand back to the steering wheel. She straightened in the seat as her heart thumped a warning. The fatigue fled, replaced by a frisson of fear.

She flicked another gaze in the mirror. Headlights charged along the road, coming closer.

Her eyes dropped to the speedometer as her foot pushed down on the gas. Fifty-five miles per hour. Sixty.

The lights drew closer.

From their intense glare and raised elevation, the vehicle appeared to be larger than her four-door.

An SUV perhaps?

The muscles in her neck tensed. The road curved and she struggled to keep the wheels on the pavement. A gust of wind swooped through a break in the trees.

She gripped the wheel more tightly, made the turn and felt pinpricks of anxiety dance along her neck. Once again lights flashed in the mirror.

The vehicle loomed directly behind her.

Would it pass? She raised her foot off the gas to let the pickup race around her.

Instead, the truck swerved toward the edge of the road, cutting her off.

Meredith turned the wheel to the right. Her front tire left the asphalt. She fought to keep the vehicle from slipping off the shoulder, but lost control.

The car plunged into the drainage ditch, slamming against the far side of the embankment.

With a whoosh, the air bag exploded against her.

Instinctively, she reached for the baby.

Oh, Lord, protect this child.

The world shifted. She closed her eyes and rested her head against the seat rest, trying to stave off vertigo.

Rubbing her stomach, she was rewarded with a fairly substantial kick to her inner abdomen.

Thank You, God.

The baby had come through the crash unharmed.

Now to focus her attention on the next problem. How to untangle herself from the air bag.

She pushed the yards of lifeless fabric to the side

and reached for the car door as the sound of another door opening drew her attention.

A steel-gray pickup with an extended cab and tinted windows sat on the side of the road. A man draped in shadow walked around the back of the truck.

Clawing at her door, Meredith tried to push it open, then threw her full weight against the resistant metal.

"Please," she moaned. Currents of fear zigzagging down her spine.

She unbuckled her seat belt and raised her leg to climb over the console. Surely the passenger-side door would open. But with the baby wedged against the steering wheel, she couldn't move.

Again, she pushed on the driver's-side door, her eyes riveted on the man who walked resolutely toward her car.

If she screamed, who would hear her? She needed to protect herself and her child.

Her hand touched the knife in her pocket.

Frantically, she opened the blade.

Holding it in her right hand, she turned to face the door.

The man stepped closer. Short black hair, wide eyes, stubble that lined his chin. Even in the shadows, she could see the sneer that tugged at his lips.

Her heart pounded relentlessly against her chest, warning her of the danger. As if she needed a warning.

He reached for the door handle and chuckled, a deep, maniacal sound that sent another bevy of chills rolling through her body.

Meredith hid the knife in the folds of her sweater.

"Looks like you were trying to run away." He pulled the door open and reached for her arm.

Meredith lunged. The knife slashed into his flesh.

He cried in pain and drew back.

She stabbed the air, hoping to force him away from the car so she could climb out and run for cover.

Initially, her jab had caught him off guard. Now he was focused completely on her. His hand crashed into her shoulder. She screamed as pain slammed through her.

He caught her wrist in a viselike grip, forcing the knife to drop from her fingers.

Anger blazed in his eyes.

He stooped, picked up the knife and raised his hand to strike.

FIVE

After Meredith's hasty retreat on the beach, Pete grabbed his bag, left the motel room, climbed into his Jeep and headed north, following her car's taillights. No telling where she was going this time of night.

She'd claimed she needed space. In his mind that meant time alone to process the information he'd piled on her slender shoulders.

If that's what she wanted, so be it. He'd hang back, letting her think she was on her own, all the while keeping her car in view.

Except he'd lost sight of her a couple miles back.

Just so long as she didn't turn off the main road.

Surely, once he rounded the curve ahead, he'd catch sight of her again. At least, he hoped he would.

Pete clutched the wheel and made the turn.

His heart slammed into his throat. Meredith's car sat nose down in a deep ravine. A man stood by the driver's door, hand raised, ready to strike.

Pete swerved to the side of road and sprang from the Jeep.

"No!" he screamed. Adrenaline pumping, hands flailing, he raced headlong down the steep incline.

The guy jumped back and scurried up the hill away from Pete.

As much as he wanted to slam his fist into the guy's jaw, Pete's first concern was Meredith.

The punk climbed into his pickup and drove out of sight.

Pete neared Meredith's car. His gut tightened as he spotted the deflated air bag spilling out of the open door, droplets of blood splattered across the fabric.

"Meredith?"

He saw movement, and relief swept over him.

She was alive.

"Pete?"

He leaned into the car and touched her shoulder. "Are you okay?"

She grimaced and tried to smile.

"What hurts?"

"Maybe everything."

He worked his hands down her arms then checked her knees and ankles. "Anything broken?"

"No. Really, I'm okay."

He dug in his pocket for his BlackBerry. "I'll call 911 for an ambulance and the police."

She grabbed his hand, her eyes wide. "Don't call anyone."

"But the baby?"

"I felt movement after the crash."

He pointed to the splatter pattern. "There's blood, Meredith. You're injured."

She shook her head. "It's not my blood. Now get me out of here."

Evidently, she'd fought back. Good for her.

He spied the knife on the ground, stooped to retrieve it and placed it in her outstretched hand.

"Any idea who that guy was?"

She bit her lip.

"Come on, Meredith. No more secrets. What's going on?"

"I…I'm not sure."

"You need the police."

She shook her head. "Please, Pete, believe me. Involving the police will just cause more problems."

"What aren't you telling me?"

"Trust me. Okay?"

"On the beach tonight, you said I didn't know a thing about you. Now you're asking me to trust you?"

"I don't have anyone else."

The truth in her words gripped his heart. Alone, pregnant, on the run. He couldn't turn his back on her now. Besides, she was Eve's daughter. Despite everything that had happened, Eve had been there when he'd needed someone growing up.

Reaching across the wheel, Pete turned off the engine and pulled the key from the ignition.

"Easy does it," he cautioned, supporting her as she pivoted in the seat and dropped her legs to the ground.

Her knees gave out when she tried to stand. He wrapped his arm more tightly around her shoulders. "There's no hurry. Let's take it one step at a time."

Her head dropped against him, her hair spilling over his chest. Her closeness stirred him.

He rubbed her shoulder, continuing to hold her. "You should see a doctor."

"Who'd have to notify the police. I told you, I don't want them involved."

Pete grumbled under his breath. "At least let me check the baby's heartbeat. I worked as a medic for a while in the army and keep a first aid kit in my Jeep."

"Thank you." She squeezed his hand then pointed back to her car. "Would you mind grabbing my purse, and there's a tote bag in the trunk."

Pete retrieved both, then helped her up the hill and eased her into the passenger seat of his Jeep. Once she was settled, he pulled the first aid kit from the rear and held the stethoscope to her belly, hearing the rapid beat of a healthy fetus. "Baby's heart sounds fine."

She dropped her head against the seat rest and sighed. "Thank God."

Noting her pallor, Pete grabbed a bottle of water from behind the seat, twisted off the cap and offered it to her.

Meredith took two long swigs before glancing up, her brow raised. "So why'd you follow me?"

He smiled. "I don't give up when something's important."

"You probably thought I was running away."

"Weren't you?"

"Maybe, but not from you."

"Eve can help, Meredith. Don't let your pride get in the way."

As soon as the words escaped his mouth, he was struck by a sense of déjà vu. Veronica had said the same thing yesterday in regard to his funding.

"Pride has nothing to do with it, Pete."

"Talking might help." Not that he practiced what he preached.

Meredith stared at him for a long moment, then placed the water bottle in the console.

"When I was eleven, I told my adoptive father I wanted to be with my real mother."

"And his reaction?"

"He took off his belt and beat me, which was his usual response to opposition."

She swallowed hard. "As much as the belt hurt, his words stung more. He said she lived in a beautiful house with servants and pretty clothes and she could do anything she wanted because she didn't have me."

Meredith studied her hands. "That night, I decided if my mother didn't want me, then I didn't want her either."

"What he said was a lie, Meredith. Your mother wanted to keep you, and she wants to reconnect with you now."

Meredith looked up at him, and her troubled eyes cut through to his heart. "Then why'd she wait so long to try to find me?"

"Because she thought you were in a good place."

Before he could say anything else, Meredith gasped. He followed her gaze. Headlights stabbed the night, coming toward them.

"He's back," she whispered.

Pete glanced at her auto, angled into the ditch. Anyone passing by would probably notify the police.

Not what Meredith wanted.

"We need to get out of here." Pete slammed the passenger-side door and rounded the Jeep. Sliding behind the wheel, he started the engine and made a U-turn heading back to Refuge Bay.

"I saw a turnoff about a quarter of a mile down the road." He hoped his voice belied the growing concern that rumbled through his gut.

A deserted road at this time of night. Did the headlights belong to the guy in the pickup?

Better not to take any chances, especially when it came to Meredith.

Pete needed to find a place to hole up where she would feel safe. Maybe then he could convince her to come with him to Atlanta. As far as he knew, nothing tied her to Refuge Bay except an abandoned bungalow and a part-time job at a quilt shop.

Eve could offer her a new life, security, even love.

If only Meredith would be more forthcoming about the man who'd run her off the road.

Meredith tried to focus on everything that had happened, but she couldn't get past the gut-wrenching dread that settled over her. The thug had come after her once again and tried to do her harm.

This time, too close for comfort.

All she wanted was peace and quiet and a chance to catch her breath.

She glanced at Pete. His hands clenched the steering wheel, and his eyes flicked back and forth from the road ahead to the reflection of the approaching vehicle in the rearview mirror.

Meredith looked over her shoulder. The headlights continued to draw closer, but with Pete at the wheel, she felt more secure.

His attentiveness to her needs and his concern for her child eased some of the questions she'd had about him earlier.

Pete seemed like a genuinely compassionate guy. Decisive. Strong-willed, but in a good way. With a take-charge attitude that she liked. As if he could handle any problem.

Something she hadn't felt with her husband.

Ben had been her saving grace after she'd run away from her adoptive father. Compared to the life she'd been living, being with Ben seemed like paradise. Free of the oppression and abuse, she'd been renewed with hope that her life would continue to improve.

But seven months ago, Ben had made a foolish mistake that changed everything. Shortly thereafter, he'd been murdered, and she'd been on the run.

At the next intersection, Pete turned inland. A

row of cottages edged the road. The last house sat dark, a FOR SALE sign in the front yard.

He pulled onto a gravel drive that led to the backyard, where he cut the lights, turned off the engine and lowered the window.

The sound of a car engine, gaining speed along the main road, filtered in with the night air. Wheels screeched, signaling that the car had taken the curve at an accelerated rate, followed by another gear shift and more acceleration until the sound faded into the distance.

Only then did Pete let out the breath he'd evidently been holding and turn to face her.

Cool air swept past him, carrying the faint scent of his aftershave. "Whoever it was stayed on the main road headed south. Might be a good reason to drive north. We can pick up I-95 in about ten miles and get something to eat, fill the car up with gas, maybe later get a couple of rooms in a motel to hole up in for the night. Unless you've got a better idea."

"That sounds fine."

Pete turned the key in the ignition and retraced their route. When they passed her car, still angled into the ditch, he said, "You'll have to call a repair shop in the morning."

She sighed. "I should have thought of that earlier. My neighbor in Refuge Bay moonlights out of his garage as a mechanic. He might be working tonight."

Pulling her cell from her pocket, she tapped in the digits and waited until the call went to voice mail. "Larry, it's Meredith. My car ran off the road." She gave the location. "I'm okay, but I need a tow. If you've got room, park it in your garage. I don't want the police asking questions."

"Everyone in your neighborhood against the cops?" Pete asked once she disconnected.

"Just Larry. I'll try him again in the morning."

She settled back in the seat. "Thanks for helping me."

"Happy to be of service, ma'am."

She couldn't resist the urge to smile. "So we get to I-95 and then find food?"

"I'll bet you skipped dinner."

And lunch, she failed to add, pulling the water bottle to her lips again. "If it were just me, I'd pass. But I need to think of the baby."

His eyes settled ever so briefly on her protruding abdomen. "When are you due?"

"In eight weeks."

His eyes widened ever so slightly. "That soon, huh? You got it all worked out? The doctor, hospital, that sort of thing?"

She shook her head. "I travel light. In fact, I don't

have baby clothes or diapers or a car seat to take the baby home from the hospital." She laughed ruefully. "At this point, I don't even have a car."

"You've still got time," he said, seemingly with conviction, which she appreciated. But they both knew he was just trying to reassure her.

Babies were needy creatures. Clothing, diapers, car seats. A stable home life. None of which she could offer her child.

Eight weeks. Saying it out loud made the time loom even closer.

And what about Pete? Would he be long gone by then? Or helping some other woman who needed a knight in shining armor?

Meredith couldn't rely on him. She'd handled situations in the past on her own. She would handle them in the future as well.

Besides, she'd asked God to help her.

She rubbed her hand over her belly. Hopefully, He wouldn't let her down.

SIX

They picked up I-95 exactly where Pete had said and headed north for twenty miles before he felt a bit more confident that they could let down their guard.

Meredith said little, but every time he glanced her way, a feeling welled up within him. A mix of protectiveness and need that filled his heart with an overwhelming desire to safeguard the innocence he saw in her eyes and knew she carried in her womb.

In the distance, an all-night roadside café sat on the top of a knoll next to a gas station where he could fill up. He pulled into a parking spot at the side of the restaurant and held the door for Meredith as they entered the outer alcove and stepped toward the dining area.

"Be with you in a minute, folks," the waitress behind the counter said in greeting.

They passed up the window seats and headed for a booth in the rear. Meredith sank into the bench seat, weariness evident in her eyes when she looked at Pete from across the table.

"Breakfast sound okay?" he asked.

"Hot tea and toast will be fine."

Pete ordered a three-egg omelet, hash browns, biscuits and gravy and a slice of Virginia ham.

He nodded toward Meredith. "Bring the lady a bowl of fresh fruit, orange juice, scrambled eggs and biscuits and ham."

His lips eased into a smile when the waitress left. "You need something substantial. Doctor's orders."

"Doctor?" The corner of her mouth twitched. "I thought you worked in a lab?"

He winked. "Even lab techs know the importance of good prenatal nutrition."

She didn't argue and ate ravenously once the food was served.

"I'll pull the car up to the gas pump," Pete said after he downed his third cup of coffee. "Finish up, and we'll meet outside."

"Sure you want to leave me alone?" she said, a hint of a tease in her voice. "Aren't you afraid I'll run away?"

He was glad to see the spark of levity, a good

sign, and he played along. "I trust you, okay? Besides, you can call me on my cell if you run into a problem. You know my number."

She stabbed another bite of ham and shoved it into her mouth. Then she flashed a see-I'm-doing-what-you-said smile that had him chuckling as he paid the bill and drove to the gas pumps.

After he filled the tank up, his BlackBerry rang.

Not a voice mail, but a photo. Pete punched the prompts and the picture downloaded across his screen.

He laughed. Meredith must like to play games.

She'd taken a photo of her empty plate.

Still chuckling under his breath, he checked the oil and washed the windows, taking his time.

Evidently, Meredith was doing the same.

Perhaps she was walking around a bit to get her circulation going. Not a bad idea at seven months.

Pete paid the attendant and eyed the restaurant. A pickup sat out front. The same make and model as the truck that had run her off the road.

His mind told him not to be concerned, but his heart didn't get the message.

Suppose something had happened? Her pregnancy, possible VHL, add adrenal tumors and a close brush with death to the list.

His muscles tensed.

Pete ran toward the restaurant, pulled open the door and stepped inside, his eyes darting back and forth. Where was she?

The ladies' restroom was located at the end of the entrance hall. He glanced into the dining area. Two men sat at the counter, their backs to the door.

An elderly couple followed Pete inside. The man headed for the dining area while the woman stepped toward the restroom.

"Ma'am? I'm traveling with a woman who's seven months pregnant, and she may not feel well." Pete pointed to the ladies' room. "If she's in the restroom, would you tell her I'm waiting for her?"

The woman raised her brow, but didn't comment as she stepped into the ladies' room.

Within seconds, the door reopened and she peered out. "No one's in here."

Anxiety tugged at Pete. Meredith had joked about running away. Surely, she hadn't taken off on her own?

His eyes scanned the nearby wooded area, hoping to spot some sign of her as he hustled back to the gas station. He'd drive around the property and see if he could find her, maybe in the picnic area nestled in front of the clump of trees at the end of the access road.

As he neared his Jeep, he caught sight of her bottom half poking out of the open door of a minivan. Untangling herself from the car, Meredith spied him and smiled.

"I made a new friend in the restaurant." She pointed to a woman who waved from the rear seat of the van. "She was getting milk for her kids and needed some help. We took the long way around the gas station back to her car."

Pete peered inside and counted three kids, none of whom looked school age.

"Can I help?" he asked.

"You must be the lucky father-to-be. Congratulations." The woman hefted a toddler into his arms. "Hold Taylor while I buckle Madison into her car seat."

The child eyed Pete warily.

"Hey there, little guy."

Taylor blinked twice, then wrapped his chubby arms around Pete's neck. "Da-Da?"

The woman laughed. "No, honey. You'll see Daddy once his plane lands."

"Janet's husband is flying into Hunter Army Airfield after a thirteen-month deployment." Meredith reached for the tired and cranky big sister who clutched a baby doll almost as tall as she was.

Taylor nuzzled Pete's neck, bringing a smile to his lips. He liked the feel of holding a child in his arms. The little tyke was a solid lump of love.

What had Janet said? Lucky father-to-be?

She'd jumped to the wrong conclusion.

Not that Pete objected.

He looked at Meredith, who was busy distracting the little girl with questions about her doll.

A strange feeling spread through Pete that had nothing to do with the toddler and everything to do with Meredith.

Spunky and determined, she made him laugh in spite of her problems. Plus, she was beautiful and, from what he'd seen so far, would make a good mom.

Too bad she'd have to raise her little one without help. Every child needed a dad. But the thought of another guy moving into Meredith's life pricked at Pete's good mood.

Truth be told, he wouldn't mind taking on the job of surrogate dad himself. Although he wasn't sure Meredith would approve.

She tickled the little girl's tummy, and the sound of their laughter flowed over Pete, along with the memory of his empty apartment and the nights he came home to nothing except a frozen pizza or fast-food burgers and fries.

Once the three kids were buckled into their car seats, the woman waved goodbye and aimed the minivan toward the interstate.

Pete was silent as he and Meredith climbed back into his Jeep.

Something had changed. A closed door deep within his core had cracked open. A door he'd kept sealed off from the world.

Being with Meredith and the nice family on their way to reconnect with their military dad had made him even more aware of the void in his own life.

His career and his research were usually all that mattered to him.

But, right now, more than anything else, Pete longed for a family of his own.

Tired as she was, and despite the hypnotic hum of the tires over the road as Pete drove through the night, Meredith couldn't sleep.

Her emotions were getting ahead of her. Probably the nesting instinct triggered by that sweet family at the gas station. At least those children had a father. But what about her baby?

She glanced at Pete. His right hand gripped the wheel, his left lay against the armrest. He sat straight, his eyes focused on the road.

As concerned as he'd been about her health and the safety of her baby, she had little doubt that he'd make a great dad. Watching him hold the toddler in his arms had confirmed that fact.

Plus he'd gone out of his way to help her—a woman he'd only just met. Initially, she thought his actions were based on his relationship with Eve, but what he'd done had gone beyond helping a friend.

For an instant, she wished she could be the woman who someday would capture his heart.

Although as little as she knew about him, Pete could already have a special someone. If there *was* another woman in his life, she certainly was one lucky lady.

"Savannah's not far. We'll stop there."

Pete turned to catch her gaze. Their eyes met, jolting her equilibrium.

"I'm okay," she quickly answered, trying to cover up the mixed signals her body was sending her.

"You keep saying that, Meredith, but you need to rest. Think of the baby."

As if she thought of anything else.

"There's a woman I know," he said. "She'll take us in."

"An old girlfriend?"

The question slipped out without forethought. Meredith and Pete had only just met, yet helping the woman at the rest stop had united them in a common goal and filled her with a sense of connection. Something else stirred within her. A heightened attraction to the man sitting in the driver's seat.

"Actually, she's a friend of Eve's," Pete answered.

Meredith shook her head. "I told you, I don't want to see my mother."

"Understood." He glanced her way, his eyes filled with compassion.

"Sheila started the VHL Institute years ago to help her son who had the disease. Eve worked with her." Pete shrugged. "They were old friends from grammar school days."

"How's her son?"

Pete let out a lungful of air. "Brice died eight months ago."

Back to reality. Forget what had happened at the rest stop.

Meredith's buoyed spirit deflated with the realization of the seriousness of the disease she could have and could then pass on to her baby.

Sheila had tried to save her son and failed.

What about Eve? Was she trying to save Meredith or merely assuaging her own guilt?

Pete insisted that Eve had thought she was doing what was best for her baby girl when she'd given Meredith up for adoption.

If only she could believe him.

"It's the middle of the night, Pete. We can't just knock on someone's door and say we need a place to stay."

"Yeah, we can. Sheila's a great lady. You'll like her."

And you'll like your mother, she waited for him to add. But Pete turned his attention back to the road.

Meredith rested her head against the seat. She had to admit that she was tired. Exhausted was a more accurate description.

She'd gratefully accept the woman's hospitality for one night. But in the morning, she'd take off on her own.

What would she tell Pete? Thanks for all your help, but I'll go it alone from now on?

Maybe she'd leave when he wasn't watching. Meredith hated being secretive after he'd done so much for her, but she had to protect her baby, and going to Atlanta wasn't on her agenda right now. Sometime in the future, when she had her feet on the ground, and she and the baby were doing okay, then she could consider reconnecting with her mother.

But Pete had said Eve was dying. If she waited too long, she'd miss the opportunity to see the woman who had given her life.

Pete left the north–south expressway and turned onto another thoroughfare that led into the city.

Signs of urban decline confirmed that, just like other metropolitan areas, people in Savannah worked hard to eke out a living. Rooms to rent and boarded-up storefronts were signs of the times. Not what Meredith had expected, but even Southern jewels like Savannah weren't immune to poverty and despair.

"We're almost in the historic district."

"You come here often?" she asked.

"When I was stationed at Fort Stewart with the army, I'd head for the city whenever I had a three-day pass." He smiled. "I've always loved history. You'll see some of the sights as we get close to Sheila's home. She owns an historic house just off Lafayette Square."

Pete's voice was filled with delight as he pointed out landmarks. "The riverfront…the oldest AME church in America…the Green-Meldrim House where General Sherman had his headquarters after his March to the Sea."

Despite her fatigue, Meredith could feel his excitement and for a few minutes she forgot about everything that had happened in the last few days.

He turned onto a street where gaslights flickered.

Even in the wee hours of the morning, the charm of the beautiful old homes in the historic district made her breath catch.

Pete pulled to the curb in front of a three-story Federal-style house. A wrought-iron double stairway led to the front door where a pair of bronze lions stood guard. A small front garden was awash with azaleas and cherry trees, their tiny buds bursting into bloom.

"Stay here, while I talk to Sheila." Pete left the Jeep and headed up the steps.

Meredith watched him raise the large brass knocker. The door cracked open and a woman wrapped in a terry cloth robe gave him a quick hug, then waved to Meredith.

He hustled back to the car, grabbed her overnight bag and helped her onto the sidewalk.

"Sheila's happy to put us up for the night," he said.

The gracious hostess stepped onto the porch to greet Meredith with a warm hug. "I'm so glad Pete brought you here. Your mother's a dear friend of mine. Now let's get inside. You must be exhausted. I've got a room ready. If you're hungry, I can prepare something to eat."

Sheila was about Meredith's height and probably in her mid-forties. She wore her hair in a short bob and her smile was genuine when she wrapped her arm around Meredith and walked with her into the elaborately furnished home.

A spiral staircase, thick Oriental rugs, polished hardwood floors and elegant period furniture made Meredith think of another era long ago.

"Pete, take Meredith's bag to the room at the top of the stairs. You can stay at the end of the hall, third door on the left."

Sheila showed Meredith into a room on the second floor where a poster bed covered in a thick comforter and plush pillows beckoned her forward.

"There's a basket of guest toilette supplies on the dresser. Soap, shampoo, cream. Let me know if you need anything else. Sleep as long as you can in the morning. I'll keep breakfast warm for you."

Once she was alone, Meredith stretched out on the luxurious bedding, too tired to change out of the clothes she was wearing. She pulled the comforter over her legs and started to slip into a deep sleep.

The last thing she thought of before the darkness settled was seeing Pete's face as he'd pulled her from the wrecked auto. Instead of fear, she felt longing.

SEVEN

The next morning, Pete found Sheila in the enclosed courtyard at the rear of the house. He crossed the flagstone patio to where she sat at the wrought-iron table.

"Pour yourself a cup of coffee." She indicated the silver urn on the side cart. "The basket contains pastries. I can fix eggs if you'd like something heartier."

He smiled with appreciation. "A couple croissants and coffee will be fine." Once he filled his mug, he carried his plate to the table and sat in a chair across from her.

Sheila's brow was furrowed and tiny lines creased the corners of her eyes. She looked tired and older than he remembered. Probably a result of the grief she carried from losing her son to VHL.

"I'm so sorry about Brice."

"Thanks for that nice note you sent with the flowers."

"You did everything you could for him, Sheila."

She looked down at her coffee and ran her finger over the rim of the cup. "I wanted to find a cure to save my son. That's why I started the Institute."

"You've heightened awareness. There's been more interest, more research."

"Only because of Brice and the others who suffer as he did, not from any effort on my part." She pulled her bottom lip through her teeth and shook her head ever so slightly. "It's a terrible disease that knows no boundaries. I always wished I had been the one with VHL. For the longest time, I feared he had inherited it from me."

"Eve said you were tested and didn't carry the defective gene."

"Brice was one of the few people to get VHL sporadically. 'Chosen by God,' he used to joke." Her voice caught. "I can't talk to Eve about it."

"She's strong, Sheila. Eve knows what her future holds."

"Right now, losing Brice is all the pain I can bear. I can't add any more." She looked at him across the table. "Does that make sense?"

"It's because you and Eve are so close."

"That's why I want to protect her."

Just as he wanted to protect Meredith.

Sheila's eyes were filled with questions. "Eve says her faith and her suffering make her stronger. I wish I could believe what she tells me. But it's hard. If God has the power to change lives, why didn't He cure my son?"

The same question Pete asked himself concerning Eve.

"Eve told me the dark times come from our human condition," Sheila continued. "But God can bring light into the darkness. She said Brice is now free of disease and pain and the uncertainty of when or where the next tumor will appear. He's whole and healthy and surrounded by everything good. She called it the fullness of eternal life."

"Did her words help?"

"They brought peace. I still grieve for my son, but I no longer worry about him. Can you understand that?"

"I'm not sure."

He pulled the china cup to his mouth and took a long swig of the hot coffee. What about Meredith? Did she have VHL? Would she learn that her baby was affected as well?

Seemed that a loving God wouldn't let an innocent child be stricken with a fatal condition.

"I'm not sure I can believe in anything except what I can influence, Sheila."

He glanced up at the bedroom window where Meredith was sleeping. If he couldn't save Eve, maybe his research might benefit Meredith and her unborn child.

And what about God?

Would Pete ask for His help?

Not now.

Maybe not ever.

Meredith woke to bright sunlight pouring through the window. She glanced at the clock on the nightstand. 11:00 a.m. She hadn't slept that soundly or that late in months.

Usually she lay awake for hours listening for trucks that drove too slowly, or settling floorboards that sounded like someone walking in the house, or wind that reminded her of when the police had stood at her door and told her Ben was dead.

She shook her head ever so slightly. This wasn't the time to look back.

Throwing the comforter aside, Meredith glanced out the window to the garden where Pete and Sheila were deep in conversation.

Pete sat in a band of light that filtered through the trees. A breeze ruffled the collar of his shirt. He raised his right hand for emphasis as he spoke to Sheila, his brow wrinkled, his gaze serious.

For an instant, Meredith imagined the clean scent of his aftershave and the strength of purpose she could almost hear in his voice.

Her night's rest was thanks to Sheila's generous hospitality and Pete's determination to find her a safe haven, at least for one night.

Meredith appreciated his calm persistence to ensure her well-being and was touched by his concern for her safety.

"I'll take care of you," he'd said to her.

Her adoptive father used the same words when he shoved her in the basement closet where she'd whimper with fear, not knowing if he'd ever return to set her free again.

In his twisted mind, the closet was a safe place. At least that's what her adoptive mother had claimed.

But then Hazel Collins never admitted that they lived with a psychotic man who controlled every aspect of their lives.

When Hazel died, Meredith had escaped. Forced to act because of her adoptive father's rage.

Not that she could tell Pete what had happened that night. Not that she could tell anyone.

That phase of her life was over. At least, she prayed it was.

Meredith peered outside again, her eyes drawn to Pete. Gratitude swept over her.

Savannah was far from Refuge Bay. The men would never search for her in such elegant surroundings.

She glanced around the room, unaccustomed to so many comforts. Her fingers touched the thick terry cloth towel set Sheila had placed on the dresser. She smiled. Sometimes it was nice to be spoiled.

Once Meredith was out of the shower and had changed into a comfortable pantsuit with an elastic waist that provided ample room for her growing baby, she gathered her personal items and returned them to her tote.

Picking up her cell, she tapped in the mechanic's number and left another message concerning her car.

When the repairs were completed, Meredith would make a quick trip back to Refuge Bay to pick up her automobile. Surely the thugs would have given up their search for her by then.

What did they want from her? To ensure that she wouldn't go to the police? But she had nothing to tell them.

She tucked the knife and her cell phone in her pocket and shoved her purse into her overnight bag, then zipped it shut.

Meredith planned to stash her bag downstairs by the front door. If an opportunity arose, she could slip out of the house without having to run back upstairs to retrieve her things.

A sense of optimism settled over her. Maybe it was the sunshine or the new buds bursting forth on the trees. Flowering Bradford pear trees, cherry blossoms and redbuds heralded spring and filled her with hope.

That's what Pete had provided. Hope that things would get better.

Despite Ben's murder. Despite the men who continued to surface. Despite a disease she may have inherited.

Grabbing her bag, she walked downstairs, the smooth mahogany banister cool to her touch.

She left her tote by the door, then wove her way through the perfectly decorated home until she found the open French doors that led to the well-manicured backyard.

"I'm afraid I overslept," she said, stepping into the sunlight.

Pete looked up. A smile spread across his face, causing a warm glow of acceptance to swell within her. How long had it been since anyone had greeted her with such a sincere look of welcome?

"I hope you slept well." Sheila rose from her chair. "There's juice and fresh fruit on the table. Sit next to Pete, and I'll bring out a plate of cold cuts and cheese, along with some French bread and condiments." She reached for Pete's cup. "Can I pour you a refill?"

"Thanks, Sheila, but I can get it. And don't feel you need to feed us. Meredith and I can grab lunch at one of the local restaurants."

"Don't be silly," Sheila said. "In fact, why don't you stay another night?"

Brow raised, he looked at Meredith. "Do you need more time to rest?"

"Actually, I feel great." She smiled at Sheila. "I deeply appreciate all you've done for us."

"Nonsense, it's nothing. Besides, I'm thrilled to be able to meet you at long last. You two chat while I get lunch ready."

Meredith poured juice and placed two slices of melon on a plate.

Pete helped her with her chair, then waited as she bowed her head and offered thanks. At the conclusion of the prayer, she raised her eyes to find him staring at her.

Her cheeks warmed, and she reached for her glass of orange juice to cover the unexpected flip-flop of her heart.

Pete sat back in his chair. "You look like you got a good night's sleep."

"That's because I did. You and Sheila have been so kind."

"I think Sheila enjoys having someone in the house. If we take her up on another night, we could tour the city and the surrounding area."

His eyes twinkled, revealing his deep appreciation for the city's history. "I've met so many good people here who are proud of their heritage. Many of them talk about ancestors who were slaves, often hidden in dank basements and whisked through secret tunnels just to be free."

Meredith had grown up in slavery. Not the type Pete talked about, but a slavery of control and manipulation.

She would have done anything to gain her freedom. Except crawl through a narrow underground tunnel.

Death paled in comparison to the terror confined places still held for her.

Thanks to Sam Collins.

Sheila appeared, carrying a large tray of food. "Lunch is ready," she sang out, arranging the assortment of cold cuts and cheese on the table where Meredith and Pete sat.

Throughout the meal, their conversation focused on Savannah and the charm of the historic district. Meredith ate heartily, surprising herself with her appetite. She was equally surprised at how comfortable she felt sitting next to Pete, as if she'd known him for a lifetime.

After they finished, Sheila scooted her chair back from the table and patted Meredith's arm. "I may be butting in where I shouldn't, but as I told you, Eve and I are friends."

Sheila pursed her lips. "You know about her medical condition, and I'm sure Pete mentioned the importance of being tested for VHL. If you feel up to it, he could draw your blood today and send it out to the lab we use so you can have the results that much sooner."

Before Meredith could comment, Sheila turned to Pete. "You can get everything you need at the Institute. It's not far from here. Barbara McSwain is on duty today. I can call ahead and let her know you're coming."

Much as Meredith wasn't ready to be tested, if Pete left the house, she could bid goodbye to Sheila and disappear into the city while he was gone.

Last night she had spied a number of ROOM-TO-RENT signs in the older section. She also recalled seeing a public health clinic where she could get prenatal care.

"That sounds like a good idea," Meredith said, hoping her enthusiasm didn't seem forced.

Sheila stepped inside to make the phone call while Pete leaned across the table and reached for her hand.

"You're making the right decision," he said. "Adrenal tumors could come into play during delivery. If your doctor knows what to expect, you'll be in less danger."

She pulled her hand back. "Danger?"

"High blood pressure is the main complication."

"Could it affect the baby?"

The way he shrugged off the question was more telling than if he'd used medical jargon to define the problem. More good news.

"It's not something to worry about at this point," he assured her. "You may not even have the disease. That's why testing is important."

He glanced at his watch. "If I go to the Institute now, I can have your samples ready for pickup this afternoon. The sooner you know the results, the better."

Pete hurried across the stone patio and entered the house. A few seconds later, he stuck his head through the open French doors and said something to her.

But she was still trying to process this new glitch: that high blood pressure could place her baby at risk. "Pardon?"

"I said I'll put your bag in my car." He disappeared again.

Dropping her napkin on the table, she pushed her chair back and hurried after him.

"Pete?" she called out as she threw open the front door.

His Jeep was already at the end of the block. He turned left and drove out of sight.

Her plan to leave while he was at the Institute wouldn't work. Not when he had the bag that contained the baby quilt she'd made, each stitch filled with love for her unborn child.

Hopefully, she'd find another opportunity to get away later in the day.

Then, for an instant, she wondered why she'd want to leave a man who had done so much to help her.

EIGHT

The VHL Institute occupied a three-story stucco building at the western edge of the historic district. Initially, Sheila's ex-husband had owned the building and leased the property to the Institute at a reduced cost.

Four years later, the influential businessman and pillar of Savannah society had dropped dead of cardiac arrest.

Under Sheila's direction, the Institute had grown and flourished and had recently started funding research that held the promise of unlocking the secrets of VHL.

Progress had been made in understanding the disease, but more work was still needed. All too often, medical advancement came in small increments, sometimes hard to measure. The compilation of data spread over a period of years from various researchers could be the catalyst for uncovering the missing piece that would eventually lead to a breakthrough.

Pete had refused to accept Eve's help in the form of grant money from the Institute, but he appreciated the excellent work they did and the breakthroughs that had been made.

A middle-aged woman approached Pete as he stepped through the massive double doors. "Mr. Worth?"

He nodded and extended his hand. "That's right. Pete Worth."

"I'm Barbara McSwain. Sheila called and said to expect you. I'll take you to the specimen collection room where you should be able to find everything you need."

Pete appreciated Sheila calling ahead. He followed Ms. McSwain down a long corridor lined with photos of major contributors to the Institute.

Eve's picture hung in a section reserved for Lifetime Benefactors. The photo had been taken a number of years before. Her eyes sparkled, and her smile was warm. She seemed like the picture of health, exuding encouragement and hope.

How different from two days ago when Pete had seen her at the lab.

The collection room held three phlebotomy

stations and a stainless-steel cabinet containing the supplies Pete needed. He accepted the plastic biohazard bag Ms. McSwain provided and filled it with the appropriate specimen collection supplies as well as the paperwork for VHL testing.

Task completed, he thanked Ms. McSwain and headed outside.

Eve's face continued to float through his thoughts. With Meredith agreeing to be tested, surely it was time to let Eve in on the good news.

Pulling his BlackBerry from his pocket, Pete punched in her private number.

Eve answered on the fourth ring.

"I found your daughter," he said in greeting.

"Pete?"

"The woman in the photo isn't your child. Your real daughter's name is Meredith Lassiter. Right now she's with Sheila."

"You're in Savannah?"

"That's right. You know Sheila, the queen of Southern hospitality."

"But what about Dixie?"

"It's a long story. Just don't do anything until we get to Atlanta."

"You're bringing Meredith here?"

Pete didn't understand Eve's hesitation. "You wanted to find your daughter."

"That's why I hired a private investigator. He assured me Dixie Collins *is* my daughter."

"What about DNA testing?"

"She's traveling and can't be reached. The P.I. said Dixie would provide a specimen as soon as she gets home."

Pete drew the BlackBerry closer to his ear. Eve was being duped by the woman, and the private investigator could be in on the scam as well.

"The P.I.'s lying. I saw Dixie Friday night. She and her boyfriend led me to Meredith. The P.I. must be involved with them. They're trying to con you, Eve."

"The private investigator was well recommended," she insisted.

"Just as Sam and Hazel Collins were?"

He heard her quick intake of breath, then silence. Pete had hit a nerve, but Eve needed to know the truth. She and her parents had trusted a lawyer to find a good home for her daughter long ago. Meredith's reaction when Pete had mentioned Sam and Hazel Collins proved that the wealthy family had made a mistake then.

Pete couldn't let Eve make another mistake now.

"You've got to believe me, Eve. Meredith is your daughter."

When Eve failed to respond, the memory of all

that had happened so long ago threatened to explode.

Ever since the first time he'd seen Eve at Magnolia Medical, Pete had tried to contain the frustration that bubbled close to the surface.

"You don't believe me and worse than that, you don't trust me. That's it, isn't it, Eve?"

"Pete, please."

"Your parents said I wouldn't amount to anything. The apple never falls far from the tree. Wasn't that the phrase they used?"

"They were upset."

"Upset? They kicked my father and me off the estate. I was twelve years old."

He glanced around at the lazy street with the regal homes. Wealth and prestige. What Eve's family had and his father always wanted.

Pete shook his head. Why was he opening himself up to relive the pain of the past after he'd kept it buried for so long? This wasn't the time or the place.

But one question haunted him. "Why didn't you try to see me again?"

"Oh, Pete, I tried. It took me a few weeks, but when I found your father, he forbade me to have contact with you."

"So you did nothing?"

"I…I gave him money each month."

Pete couldn't believe what he heard. "My father accepted your money?"

"There were things you needed that he couldn't provide. I knew times were tough."

An understatement. They'd gone from a comfortable lifestyle on the estate to a hand-to-mouth existence that had taken every ounce of determination to survive. His father had chosen the easy way out. He'd turned to the bottle for relief.

Now Pete realized where he had gotten the money to buy the booze.

"You didn't help me. Don't you see, Eve, you made it worse. Your money enabled my father to become consumed by a disease that eventually killed him. All the while, I was studying to research a cure for yours."

He pressed the disconnect button, his insides churning with anger and frustration.

His father had accepted money from Eve, all the while continuing to fill his only son with hate for the wealthy family who had cast them out from their home.

Pete had known his father had a warped sense of right and wrong, but he hadn't thought the old man had been so far off base. Now the reality of what and who his father had been hit him in the gut.

He wanted to scream to the heavens and ask the

God Eve claimed was so merciful why people twisted love and made it so destructive? Why children were innately programmed to believe they were loved, despite the outward signs that smacked of manipulation and control.

If his father were still alive, Pete would demand to know the truth. Could Eve be right?

All these years, Pete had harbored resentment against her and her parents. Now he realized that he should have reserved some of that anger and resentment for his own dad.

Pete jerked open the door of his Jeep and slid behind the wheel. Too many emotions swirled through his mind.

He needed to push them aside for now. Bury them, as he had done for so long.

Someday he would try to make sense of what Eve had just told him.

But, right now, he had a woman waiting for him. A wonderful woman who needed his help, despite Eve's hesitation to accept Meredith as her daughter.

He wouldn't let Meredith down. Not like his father, who seemed to have let everyone down. Not like the Townsends, who had banished a little boy and his father from their home. Not like Eve, who had failed to follow him and now failed to accept that Meredith might be her legal heir.

Eve had given his father money. Wasn't that the answer the rich always provided? Fix a problem with their wallets.

At least she'd done something, his voice of reason whispered.

But it hadn't been enough then, and it wasn't enough now to right the wrongs of the past.

Meredith stood on the front porch looking for a glimpse of Pete's car. So much for her plans to leave while he was at the Institute. The baby quilt she'd painstakingly stitched over the last few months was too precious to leave behind.

She'd abandoned so much already.

Abandoned. The word hit her with force.

Destructive. Intimidating. Extracting every shred of self-worth she'd worked so hard to build, like a powerful tsunami when the waters pulled back from the shoreline. She grasped the door, waiting for the incoming wave that always followed. With it would flow the fear and memory of her cries for help as, once again, she was that little girl locked in the darkness.

The baby moved in her womb, forcing her back to the present.

Meredith looked through the doorway into the house and saw the sunlight filtering through the large Palladian windows.

Light not darkness.

God is the light of the world.

The infant she carried—her child—was her hope for the future.

She had to move forward.

Setting her jaw with determination, Meredith stepped over the threshold and walked toward the light.

She found Sheila clearing the lunch dishes and hastened to gather the rest of the plates and silverware off the table. "The least I can do is help. You've been so kind."

The older woman's smile stretched across her oval face. "This house is far too large and too lonely for one woman. Having you here has brightened my day to say the least."

They carried the dishes into the kitchen and loaded the dishwasher. Once the task was completed, Sheila rinsed her hands in the sink and wiped them on a paper towel.

"It's been good reconnecting with Pete. I haven't seen him in a number of years."

"He said he knew your son."

Sheila nodded. Her smile turned poignant. "Brice and I visited the estate often. Eve seemed so happy back then, despite the disease."

"When did you first learn Brice had VHL?"

"We were at the beach." Sheila leaned against the counter. "I noticed a knot on his back. The doctor said it was probably nothing, but he sent us to a specialist just to be sure."

Sheila stared out the large windows that lined one wall of the kitchen. A hummingbird fluttered outside, its narrow beak drawing sugary nectar from a feeder.

"When he was little, Brice was as energetic as that hummingbird. Turns out he was just as fragile. Eventually, his eyes were affected. Slowly, progressively, his vision faded until he could see nothing except the very brightest light."

A squirrel skittered down a giant oak, frightening the hummingbird, which drew back from the feeder and flew away.

"I called Brice my shining star." Sheila rubbed her hands over her crossed arms. "Funny the names we mothers call our children."

Meredith thought of the words she used for her child: precious one, buttercup, sweet pea.

"I never thought the light of my life would be extinguished so early."

Sheila shook her head as if shaking free of the memories. "But we were talking about Pete." She forced a smile. "Eve always considered him the son she never had."

"I didn't know their relationship was that close."

"*Was* is the key word." The older woman pulled in a breath. "Pete should be the one to tell you, but of course he won't. He's too private. Probably too proud. But I've seen the way he cares for you, Meredith."

Her hand grasped the countertop. She hadn't expected Sheila's comment or the warmth that fluttered through her body.

"Pete's dad worked as caretaker on Eve's parents' estate," Sheila said. "He was a surly man, and the Townsends eventually asked him to leave."

"And Pete?"

"Was caught between his father and the woman who had cared for him like a mother."

"What about his own mother?" Meredith asked.

"She hemorrhaged giving birth." Sheila shook her head. "We sometimes forget that childbirth can be life-threatening, despite modern medical science."

Heat seared through Meredith, this time brought on by the premonition of what could happen. What had Pete said? VHL could lead to complications during delivery.

Sheila continued, oblivious to the impact her words had on Meredith. "Pete's mother's death added to his father's ill will toward his wealthy landlords. Seemingly, in his mind, only good followed Eve and her family, while his life was mired in misery."

"Sounds like a very unhappy man," Meredith managed to mumble, trying to focus on Pete's past and not the medical complications that could compound her delivery weeks from now.

Sheila raised her brow. "And not one easily prone to show love for his only child."

Meredith's heart went out to Pete, whose youth had to have been difficult. Children needed to be surrounded by affection and goodness, not misery and grief. She knew that only too well.

"Pete said Eve's parents forced her to give me up for adoption."

Sheila reached out and rubbed her hand over Meredith's shoulder. "She was young. Of course, Eve would comply with her parents' wishes. Her only comfort was knowing her child had been adopted by a loving family."

A lump of bitterness filled Meredith's throat. "Undoubtedly, she thought she was doing the right thing."

Sheila eyed Meredith as if hearing the ring of disbelief in the statement. "We all make mistakes."

"Only some cause more damage than others." Meredith ran her hand over her face. "For some reason, I'm feeling a bit tired."

"Why don't you find a comfortable chair in the

sunroom and curl up with a magazine. I have some work I need to do in the study."

Sheila led her through the kitchen to a delightful room filled with windows that overlooked the garden. Bright chintz fabric decorated the overstuffed furniture in a royal blue-and-yellow plaid that invited Meredith to sit and relax. Something she wasn't accustomed to doing. While the rest of the house was decorated in period furnishings, this room was country chic and inviting.

"Can I bring you a cup of tea?"

"Maybe later. Thank you, Sheila."

Meredith settled back into the plush cushions. She raised her legs onto the matching ottoman and closed her eyes as the bright sunshine poured through the expansive windows.

Totally relaxed, Meredith let her mind drift. The sound of Sheila tinkering in the study seemed like a natural backdrop.

Despite her restful sleep last night, Meredith dozed.

Her mind filled with thoughts of Pete and, off in the distance, a woman whose face was blurred in the haze of the dream.

"Meredith...Meredith..."

Voices pulled her from her slumber.

Sheila's was raised in question. "What are you doing?"

A man's baritone—insistent and heavily accented—shouted back at her.

Meredith rose from the chair.

A movement caught her eye in the garden. The cold, tight grip of fear clamped down on her heart.

A man stood on the patio.

Medium height. Dark hair. Eyes that glared at her through the glass.

She slapped her hand against her pocket, found her cell phone and inadvertently opened the CALLS SENT file.

Pete's number was highlighted.

She punched the green button.

Sheila screamed from the living room.

Meredith's hands seemed stiff as claws, and she almost dropped the small device before raising it to her ear.

Why was the connection taking so long?

She glanced once again at the phone just as it began to ring.

When she looked back into the garden it was empty.

Footsteps sounded in the hallway outside the sunroom.

"Hello?" Pete's voice.

"The man who ran me off the road is in Sheila's house."

NINE

Pulse pounding, Pete navigated the restful historic district at mach speed. The brakes screeched in protest as he turned onto Sheila's street and swerved to the curb in front of the three-story home. Leaping to the sidewalk, he took the stairs to the front porch two at a time and reached for the brass knob.

The door swung open.

Sheila lay on the Oriental carpet in the entryway. A pool of blood soaked the rug, turning the elaborate pattern a monochromatic magenta. The smell of copper filled the hallway. Her face was pale as death. Her arms lay at her side, hands curled inward.

He stooped to touch her neck. A pulse. Faint, but she was alive.

"Sheila, it's Pete."

Her eyes flickered open. "Mere…dith?"

"Where is she, Sheila?" He lowered his face to hers, hoping to hear her response.

Her eyes closed.

He nudged her shoulder. "Sheila?"

Blood oozed from a gash in her side. He grabbed a woolen throw from a nearby chair and bundled it around the wound to stop the bleeding. A makeshift tourniquet at best, but the flow of blood eased.

Stumbling to his feet, he ran to the study.

"Meredith!" he screamed.

Grabbing the house phone, he punched 911 and raced on to the living room.

The doors to the garden stood open.

He flicked his gaze over the well-maintained courtyard, searching for some sign of her.

The emergency response operator's voice sounded in his ear.

"There's been a break-in," he hastened to explain. "A woman's bleeding heavily from what appears to be a knife wound to her right side." Pete gave the address. "She's got a pulse, but it's faint. Send an ambulance and the police. Tell them to hurry."

"How would you describe her condition, sir?"

Pete didn't have time for this. He had to find Meredith. "Look, lady, she's barely alive. I need an ambulance and police now."

He threw the phone onto a nearby couch and ran up the stairs to the second floor. The room where Meredith had slept was empty.

Next he checked the master suite, then Brice's old room and the fourth bedroom where Pete had stayed. The deadly silence heightened the sound of his own heart pounding in his ears.

Mouth dry, he flew down the stairs to the sunroom.

A circular table next to one of the overstuffed chairs lay overturned. A lamp had shattered on the hardwood floor. Spying something under the coffee table, he stooped and retrieved the pocketknife Meredith had used last night.

Clutching it in his hand, he retraced his steps to the entry where Sheila lay and knelt next to her.

Her eyes blinked open.

"Hold on, Sheila. Help's on the way."

"At…lan…ta," she whispered, her voice raspy.

"What?"

"Two men. They…they…" She licked her lips. "Buckhead."

The trendy, upscale area north of downtown. "Is that where they're taking Meredith?"

Sirens sounded in the distance.

"Find…find her."

Someone shouted. Pete stepped outside. A man ran from the house across the street.

"I phoned Sheila but didn't get an answer." Face flushed, a line of sweat spotted the portly neighbor's upper lip as he climbed the stairs. "When I saw you race from your Jeep, I thought something might be wrong."

"There's been a break-in. Sheila's been injured." Pete indicated the open entryway.

The guy neared. His eyes widened when he spied Pete's shirt. "You're covered in blood."

The neighbor glanced inside, then back at the knife Pete still held in his hand. "Oh my God, you killed her."

"She's not dead, but she needs help. The ambulance is on the way. There was another woman in the house. They've taken her to Atlanta. Tell the police I'm headed for Buckhead." Pete backed down the steps. "Stay with Sheila until the EMTs arrive."

Sirens grew louder.

Pete jumped into his Jeep and glanced at his rearview mirror. An ambulance and two police cars turned onto the block.

His BlackBerry rang.

A photo, slightly out of focus. Apparently taken while in motion through a dirt-streaked window.

A road sign. INTERSTATE 16.

Good for Meredith. She was letting him know the route her captors were taking.

Pete tramped on the accelerator. If Meredith continued to send pictures, he'd be able to find her.

He glanced once again at the blurred photo.

Or at least he hoped he would.

"God, help me," Meredith moaned as the pickup headed into the interior of the state.

Shifting her weight, she rolled onto her side to take the pressure off her baby. She hadn't felt movement since the men had knocked her out.

Dazed, she'd awakened in the enclosed bed of the pickup with a knot on her crown the size of a lemon. No doubt the reason for the throbbing pain that still threaded across her temples and down her neck. Thankfully, her vision was clear and she could move her fingers and toes.

Plus she was alive.

What about Sheila? Recalling the blood that had gushed from the woman's side as she lay in the entry alcove made Meredith's stomach roil.

Please, Lord, let her live.

She rubbed her hand over her belly. *Let my baby live, too.*

Meredith glanced through the double-paned sliding windows that separated the camper bed from the extended cab section upfront. The guy who'd run her off the road sat behind the wheel.

A second man slouched against the passenger door.

Meredith had scooted into the uppermost corner of the enclosed truck bed, hoping the men would have difficulty seeing her there.

The driver turned to the shorter man, riding shotgun. Above the sound of the engine, she heard him say, "Check on her, Javier."

Meredith closed her eyes.

The windows slid open.

A hand grabbed her shoulder and rolled her onto her back. Her head cracked against the side of the truck bed. Pain shot down her neck.

"Dead to the world, Hank." He slid the window closed and pivoted back into the passenger seat.

Meredith clenched her teeth, holding back the groan that threatened to escape from her lips.

Slowly, the pain eased.

The truck made a series of turns.

Earlier, fearing they'd hear her if she made a phone call, Meredith had raised her head and peered out the side camper window. Removing her cell from her pocket, she'd taken a photo of a road sign and sent it to Pete's BlackBerry.

Interstate 16 ran west out of Savannah toward the interior of the state and far from the coastal low country.

A succession of turns signaled that they'd changed course yet again.

Rising on her elbow and hidden from the men's view, Meredith once more peered out the side window, searching for a landmark. Something to identify the direction they were now headed.

All she could see were trees and more trees. How would anything stand out in this lonely stretch of back road to pinpoint their location?

In the distance, an old white church came into view. Two roadside historical markers sat in front of the aged structure.

She raised her cell and snapped the shot.

Dropping back to the truck bed, she glanced at the photo displayed on her cell. Only a portion of one of the markers was visible.

Her heart sank.

Much as she needed Pete, he would never be able to find her.

TEN

Interstate 16 was a well-traveled route, teeming with state patrol cars. Pete checked his speed and kept to within ten miles over the limit. Last thing he wanted was to be pulled over for a moving violation.

He *would* need law enforcement's help once he pinpointed Meredith's location. But if they stopped him now, he'd be hauled in for questioning. He didn't want delays to keep him from finding her.

Hopefully, by now Sheila would be getting the medical care she needed.

The digital clock on the dash read two minutes after the hour. He pushed the radio dial and hit SEEK until he found a Savannah station.

"New developments in the historic-district stabbing," the announcer said. "VHL Institute founder Sheila Hudson remains in critical condition

GET 2 BOOKS

IF YOU ENJOY A ROMANTIC SUSPENSE STORY that reflects solid, traditional values, then you'll like *Love Inspired® Suspense* novels. These are contemporary tales of intrigue and romance featuring Christian characters facing challenges to their faith…and their lives!

We'd like to send you two *Love Inspired Suspense* novels absolutely free. Accepting them puts you under no obligation to purchase any more books.

HOW TO GET YOUR
2 FREE BOOKS AND TWO FREE GIFTS

1. Return the reply card today, and we'll send you two *Love Inspired Suspense* novels, absolutely free! We'll even pay the postage!
2. Accepting free books places you under no obligation to buy anything, ever. The two books have combined cover prices of $11.00 in the U.S. and $13.00 in Canada, but they're yours to keep, free!
3. We hope that after receiving your free books you'll want to remain a subscriber, but the choice is yours–to continue or cancel, any time at all!

EXTRA BONUS

You'll also get two free mystery gifts! (worth about $10)

FREE!

If offer card is missing, write to Steeple Hill Reader Service, 3010 Walden Ave., P.O. Box 1867, Buffalo, NY 14240-1867

BUSINESS REPLY MAIL

FIRST-CLASS MAIL   PERMIT NO. 717   BUFFALO, NY

POSTAGE WILL BE PAID BY ADDRESSEE

Steeple Hill Reader Service
3010 WALDEN AVENUE
PO BOX 1867
BUFFALO NY 14240-9952

NO POSTAGE
NECESSARY
IF MAILED
IN THE
UNITED STATES

and is currently undergoing surgery at Riverview Hospital. An eyewitness said an overnight guest was seen running from the home. Police are looking for a white male, six feet tall and approximately 190 pounds. Anyone with knowledge of his whereabouts should contact the police."

Pete shook his head. Of course, they'd think he was involved. The neighbor had jumped to the same conclusion.

Once Pete could pinpoint Meredith's location, he'd call the authorities for help and assure them that they were searching for the wrong guy.

His BlackBerry buzzed. Pete opened the file and pulled up the photo.

The corner of a white wooden structure and a portion of a historic marker were visible. He couldn't make out the words.

Double clicking on the photo, he zoomed in. The top portion of the marker visible in the photo read, *BIG BUC,* in uppercase block letters. Underneath, he made out two words: *This church.*

Big Buc Church?

He hit the Internet icon and typed in the name. The search engine sent back an immediate reply.

Do you mean Big Buckhead Church?

"You bet I do," Pete mumbled, clicking on the first URL listed.

When Sheila heard the guys mention Buckhead, she'd thought of the upscale section of Atlanta known for fine food and late-night frivolity. Instead, they'd referred to a Civil War battle site about eighty miles from Savannah.

Big Buckhead Church...battle between Northern and Southern cavalry...Sherman's March to the Sea...Morgan County...historic marker...intersection of U.S. 25 and Big Buckhead Church Road.

Bingo!

Pete plugged the information into another program.

A map scrolled across his screen.

He was back on track. At least until Meredith sent another photo.

Meredith's heart lurched as the pickup made a sharp turn onto a gravel drive and came to a halt.

A pit stop for gas or food?

If the men thought she was unconscious, they'd leave her in the truck.

She raised her head and peered out the dirt-crusted window. A ramshackle farmhouse with a low front porch and two brick fireplaces, one on each side of the building, sat in a small clearing. Tall oaks, sweet gums and pines surrounded the house in a jungle of kudzu.

Not a filling station or fast-food restaurant in sight.

Her heart plummeted, but once again, she held her cell phone aloft. A large tree shaded the house and driveway. One of its branches jutted out at a forty-five-degree angle from the trunk.

She clicked the shot just as the men climbed from the cab, slamming the doors behind them. Sight unseen, she hastily sent the photo to Pete.

Please, Lord, let him receive the photo.

Footsteps sounded over the crushed gravel.

Meredith lowered her head, feeling the cold bed liner against her cheek.

The back hatch dropped open.

"Grab her legs."

Meredith recognized the driver's voice.

Fingers wrapped around her ankles and yanked her toward the tailgate. A raised floor bolt caught her cheek, cutting her flesh.

"Augh!" she moaned, unable to control the involuntary gasp that escaped from her lips.

"Ah, *señora*, you are finally awake." Dark skin, black eyes, coarse hair that matted against his forehead. A scar slashed across the shorter man's face.

He released her legs and dropped them to the ground. Then, grabbing her arm, he pulled her to her feet.

"You can walk, yes?"

Her knees buckled. He jerked her upright, his grip like steel on her arm. She stumbled back, crashing into the lowered tailgate.

Balance wasn't her strong suit at this point in her pregnancy, even on a good day.

"Get her inside," the driver demanded. "And be careful, Javier. She's a tiger." He glanced down at the makeshift bandage wrapped around his arm.

Meredith bristled. "I should have aimed for your throat."

Javier chuckled. "You're a little firebrand, aren't you, *señora?*"

His grip tightened as he shoved her toward the house.

If she had the knife…

But the only thing in her pocket was her cell phone.

Please, God, don't let them find it.

"What do you want with me?" Meredith demanded, trying to pull free from the Latino's hold.

"You need to learn your place, *señora*. We tell you only what we want you to hear. Your husband was a troublemaker. So are you."

"Are you working for the loan shark who owned the fishing boat and killed my husband?"

"He is in prison because of you." Javier spat out the words. "But we will make sure you do no more harm."

"The cops arrested your buddy when they realized he murdered my husband. I never divulged anything to the police, but I should have."

"Your husband knew some of them were on the take." Javier shrugged. "He learned his lesson. We will teach you as well."

The Latino pushed her up the steps and onto the wooden porch, badly in need of repair.

Grasping her arm with his left hand, Javier stuck a key in the lock with his right and opened the door.

Stale, musty air rushed past her. Meredith coughed as he shoved her inside. Layers of dust covered the hand-hewn floorboards and steep staircase leading to the second floor.

A small parlor sat to the right with a brick fireplace. Cobwebs dangled from the central light fixture. Cracks zigzagged along the plastered walls and ran across the ceiling.

Rippled antique panes of glass in the two windows—almost opaque from years of neglect—dated the aged structure.

"Sit," Javier said, ushering her toward three folding lawn chairs arranged in the center of the room. "And don't give me any back talk."

She squared her shoulders. "Seems to me only cowards would shove a pregnant woman around."

The Latino struck her face. She reeled from the blow.

"You sit down now or the next time I aim for your belly."

She gasped. *Not the baby.*

Her hand touched the back of the chair. She lowered herself into the plastic seat. This wasn't the time for defiance.

The door opened and the other man stepped inside.

"I parked the truck out back and unloaded the food." He glanced from her to Javier and raised his brow. "Trouble?"

"No way, Hank." The smug look on Javier's face belied the exchange he and Meredith had just had.

"He likes to hit women," she said, hoping to pit one guy against the other.

Hank glanced at his partner. "What Mule said was true."

Meredith raised her brow. "Is Mule as much of a coward as you are?"

His eyes narrowed. "Look, lady. We were told to bring you here, but we weren't told to keep you happy. Any more lip and you'll regret that God gave you a voice."

"At least God gave me the ability to know right from wrong."

He nodded to Javier. "Lock her up in the basement so we won't have to listen to her."

The basement? Memories flashed through her mind.

"No." She pushed back in the chair.

Javier grabbed her arm.

She fought against his hold.

His grasp tightened, but she continued to struggle.

Fight, her inner voice screamed.

She lashed out, striking his arms.

His hand crashed against her head. The room spun.

He dragged her across the floorboards. The door to the basement opened, exposing a black pit. The terrors of the past flew around her as if demons had been unleashed from their underground lair.

She screamed.

His hands shoved her forward, and she stumbled into the darkness.

ELEVEN

A maze of roads surrounded the Old Buckhead Church, giving no clue as to where Meredith could be.

The sun had been high in the sky when Pete left Savannah. Now clouds darkened the day and warned of an encroaching storm. Not what he needed.

He needed to find Meredith.

If only she would send another photo.

A memory floated through his mind. He was young, probably eight or nine. Wanting to connect with the mother he'd never known, Pete had taken her gold cross necklace from the special box in the living room and had gone outside to the rose garden where his father said his mother had liked to sit.

Lounging on the grass, Pete had closed his eyes and imagined he could feel her embrace in the warmth of the sunlight. He spent the afternoon playing in the garden until storm clouds appeared in the sky, forcing him to run home before the rain started. When he dug in his pocket for the cross, all he found was a wad of lint that had lodged there from the dryer.

Frantic, he had called Eve.

"Pray," she'd suggested. "I'll pray too. God will help you find the cross."

"Help me," Pete had pleaded with God as he ran back to the garden. Fat drops of rain fell. Frantically, he searched for the cross.

Tears burned his eyes. When he blinked them away, he saw a yellow rose—his mother's favorite color—lying on the ground. He bent down to touch the fallen petals and spied the necklace entwined among the dampened blades of grass.

Chilled and wet, Pete arrived back at the house just before his father stepped through the door, expecting the table to be set and the leftovers in the oven warming.

Pete had been spanked for not having dinner ready, but the punishment underscored what Eve had told him.

A human father's love is limited, but our Heavenly Father's love has no boundaries.

That night, he'd learned the difference.

But he was a grown man now. Could he rely on

the God of his childhood? Especially since Pete had shut Him out of his life for so long?

Pete had nowhere else to turn, and he had to find Meredith.

"Help me," Pete mumbled, his hands gripping the steering wheel.

The road narrowed, and the undergrowth in the surrounding woods thickened so that he could see nothing through the trees.

Hopelessness settled over him.

He pushed it aside.

Help me. The childlike prayer rumbled through his mind unbidden as if another had whispered the words.

At that instant, his BlackBerry rang.

He grabbed the phone and pushed the access button.

A photo appeared on the screen. A gnarled oak with a horizontal limb jutting out from the trunk, the perfect branch from which to hang a swing.

He'd seen the tree earlier as he'd maneuvered back and forth along the country road. But where?

Turning the car around, he retraced his route, trying to jar his memory. He'd been down so many roads.

Would he ever find the tree?

Would he ever find Meredith?

"Help me," he said again and again, wondering if God was listening.

* * *

Javier turned the bolt, locking Meredith in the small basement room, not much larger than a closet. She'd staggered down the steps, tripping over herself, half falling, half being dragged before he'd shoved her into this corner nook, overriding her protests and struggles to get free.

His footsteps sounded now as he climbed the stairs. Overhead, the door to the main floor slammed shut.

Meredith tried to breathe, her lungs tight from the mold and mildew that hung in the air. Threads of panic stitched their way down her spine.

A tiny window allowed a sliver of sunlight to filter into the confined area. She repositioned herself in the light, finding comfort from the rays that managed to break through the grimy glass.

Night was fast approaching.

Hopefully, she would be able to free herself before then. But how?

The only good thing about being alone in the basement was that she could finally call Pete. Pulling her cell from her pocket, she tapped in his number. The screen displayed a pinwheel of color as the system roamed for a signal, then went blank.

CALL FAILED.

Frustration and fear welled up within her. She

coughed to clear her lungs. Her back ached. The cold cement floor added to her discomfort.

Climbing first to her knees and then to her feet, she slowly and methodically worked her hands over the rough walls, hoping to find a way to escape. All she found was an old coal shovel.

How had she gotten herself into this mess?

Everything had started when the plant closed, and Ben had been out of work. Sure, they'd had problems, mainly focused on Ben's habit of spending more than they made. But he had been a good man, who was attentive and made her feel special. No one had done that before.

Somehow she'd equated that with love.

Although content, theirs had been a flawed marriage from the start.

Undoubtedly, Ben had sensed that, too. Maybe that was the reason he'd taken out the loan. Once again, he'd been too extravagant, too focused on material things.

Their problems escalated when the plant where Ben worked had closed and the thugs demanded payment. Then unexpectedly, they offered Ben a job on the fishing boat, which had seemed like the answer to Meredith's prayers.

She never realized that the men planned to make an example of Ben.

The loan sharks were a shady bunch, and her husband suspected that the cops turned a blind eye to what was happening. "Don't talk about the loan to anyone or things could get worse," Ben had warned her the night before his death.

Things *had* gotten worse. First his murder, then, while she was still reeling from Ben's death, the loan sharks had demanded the money in one lump sum. They'd upped the interest, and the final tally was far more than the original loan.

She told them she'd make good on everything after the baby was born, and once she could get a steady job.

But they weren't interested in her problems and planned to do her harm. That was why she'd run.

The light dimmed and a roll of thunder sounded outside.

She needed Pete—his strength and his determination.

Meredith pulled her cell from her pocket once again. If only she could pick up a signal. She clicked on the power source, but the screen remained black.

Pivoting toward the window, she wrapped her arms around her belly.

"Where are you, Pete?" she whispered as night fell, leaving her in darkness.

TWELVE

"Hoo-ah!"

The army cheer slipped from Pete's mouth as he spied the old oak with the swing branch. If he hadn't been searching so diligently, he would have missed the tree and the narrow path that wove back into the clearing. Peering through the foliage, he saw a two-story farmhouse, probably circa 1800, with twin fireplaces and a sagging front porch surrounded by a thick bed of kudzu. Tall pines and giant oaks tangled around the aged structure, nearly blocking any view of it from the road.

He passed by the gravel driveway and turned onto a dirt trail—hardly more than a deer path—farther down the road. Meandering back into the deep woods, he parked behind a large thicket of sweet gum trees and dense underbrush that offered protection from anyone who happened into the isolated backwoods.

Pete picked up his BlackBerry from the console and tapped in 911. Now that he'd found Meredith, he needed the help of the local police.

Pulling the mobile close, he expected to hear a ring. Instead, the pounding pulse of his own heartbeat sounded in his ear.

Lowering the phone, he glanced at the screen. His gut tightened.

No signal. No cell coverage. No way to contact the police.

Whether he liked it or not, everything rested on his shoulders. Meredith's safety—perhaps her life—depended on him. He had to succeed. He had to save her.

Pete opened his glove compartment and pulled out a Maglite. Shoving it into his pocket, he climbed from the car and picked his way through the dense forest. The outline of the farmhouse came into view on his right. He glanced left, noting the crumbling remains of an outbuilding.

Keeping undercover, Pete circled to the front of the property and hunkered down in the brush, biding his time.

A short guy, dark skin—probably Latino—stepped outside.

Wouldn't be too hard to get the upper hand on that one. What about his partner? Sheila had mentioned two men, but for all Pete knew, more could be inside.

He strained to hear some sound or snippet of conversation coming from the old farmhouse. All he could identify was the Latino's attempt to whistle in the wind.

Time to scout out the rear entrance. Slowly and methodically, Pete edged around the house to where the pickup truck sat parked beside the back stoop.

He glanced at the second-story dormer windows. If they were holding Meredith in an upstairs bedroom, he'd have to risk climbing onto the overhang that covered the porch. As old and dilapidated as the house was, the thin metal would surely buckle, the noise alerting anyone inside.

Pete dropped his gaze to what appeared to be the kitchen window. A man peered through the glass panes, looking out at the backyard.

Had he spotted Pete?

He held his breath. Any movement might catch the other man's attention.

Something slithered underfoot. Pete's neck tingled. He glanced down. A copperhead, probably three feet long, swished through the brush.

Not the time to flinch.

The face in the window retreated. Pete mentally counted to twenty-five, giving the deadly snake ample opportunity to disappear into the thicket.

Turning in the opposite direction, he retraced his steps to the outbuilding he'd seen earlier.

Recalling other pre–Civil War farmhouses, Pete knew the one room constructed of red clay brick was probably an old smokehouse or freestanding kitchen where servants had cooked food to keep the heat from the master's house in summer. Locating this building away from the main dwelling ensured that a fire sparked by grease or burning embers would never destroy what must have originally been the impressive home of a well-to-do Georgia farmer.

Focused on his target, Pete moved as silently as the snake through the thick undergrowth until he reached the outbuilding. Wiping away the film of cobwebs that barred the open doorway, he stepped onto the raised floor of the now-barren structure.

A large stone fireplace took up one wall, blackened with soot. Only a portion of the roof remained. A bird had made a nest in the crossbeams overhead and flew from its perch when Pete disrupted its solitude.

Floorboards creaked as he stepped toward a three-legged stool discarded in the corner. Pete turned it upright and lowered himself onto the seat.

Dropping his head into his hands, he closed his eyes.

How would he get inside the house to find Meredith? When he thought about her plight his gut tightened and anger bubbled up within him. Instead of focusing on her green eyes and raven hair, he needed to concentrate on how to set her free.

His first option? Make a disturbance to force the thugs outside. He could take one guy, maybe two.

But if there were more men—or if they drew their weapons—he'd be out of luck.

Which was exactly where he was right now.

Option two? Tiny windows at the base of the house established that there was a basement, which might provide an entrance. If Pete waited until night when the kidnappers slept, he could jimmy a window and gain entry without their noticing.

Thunder rumbled overhead, sounding like night fire on a maneuver range. The storm couldn't be far away.

As if on cue, raindrops splattered against the roughly hewn floor and increased in intensity until a narrow stream of water ran across the uneven floorboards.

Pete scraped his shoe over the litter of leaves and debris, noticing a raised section. Wedging his fingers between the planks, he tugged, but the boards failed to separate.

He grabbed a fallen branch from outside the

doorway and jammed the tip of the stick into the crack. Using it as a lever, he forced the planks apart and raised what appeared to be a trapdoor.

The smell of damp earth, mildew and Georgia red clay wafted past him. A cockroach scurried along the dirt and disappeared under the flooring.

A hand-hewn wooden ladder angled down into the darkness. Lightning ignited the sky, revealing a tunnel that headed in the direction of the main house.

Pete thought of the stories folks had told him about their ancestors yearning to be free. Had the old farmhouse been a stopping point on the Underground Railroad for runaway slaves journeying north? The tunnel would have provided a rapid escape route when less-than-sympathetic neighbors came calling.

If so, Pete may have found a way to reach Meredith.

Now all he needed to do was lower himself into the pit.

Hopefully the earthen walls wouldn't collapse around him.

Meredith's throat was dry and her muscles ached, but she thought little of her own discomfort. Ignoring the darkness, she focused instead on getting free.

When she'd finally gotten the courage and the opportunity to escape her adoptive father's oppressive control, she'd vowed never to allow herself to be dominated by any man again.

And never to enter confined spaces.

Too many memories returned to her now, along with the fear she'd known as a child each time Sam Collins had locked her up.

Jamming her back against the wall, Meredith drew her legs toward her chest, forming a protective cradle for her baby.

Footsteps sounded overhead. The men who had forced her into this dungeon had killed Ben and planned to kill her as well.

More footsteps, then the sound of water running and cabinets banging.

If only she could find something that would serve as a weapon.

Where was the shovel?

In the dark, she used her hands to grope over the cement floor until her fingers touched the metal handle. Clutching it to her chest, she walked around the confined area and stopped when she felt the hinges on the door. If she stood against the wall, she'd be hidden from view when it opened.

Would she be strong enough to strike a blow?

She had no choice. She had to escape.

Meredith backed into the corner. A dull pounding in her temples warned that she'd gone too long without water. Her legs cramped. She stretched out the tightness.

More movement overhead, followed by footsteps.

Another sound. Faint but persistent scratching. Perhaps a mouse or rat, scurrying to find shelter in the recesses of the basement.

As much as she didn't like rodents, they were less of a fear than the man whose footsteps pounded down the stairs.

The scratching stopped, the creature no doubt frightened by the approaching human presence.

Meredith's mouth was dry as cotton while sweat moistened her palms. She wiped one and then the other along her pants, before repositioning her fingers around the handle of the shovel. Raising it overhead, she mentally pictured herself striking a blow when the guy stepped through the door.

Her goal? To knock him out.

And then what?

She'd have to climb the stairs and face the other man. She gripped the shovel even more tightly.

Lord, I need help.

A light flipped on in the main basement area and shined through the crack under the door.

Meredith pulled in a steadying breath.

The lock clicked. The latch turned. Slowly the door opened.

"Hey, *señora*, you want some chow?"

Javier.

He stepped into the darkened interior, holding a plate of food before him.

Meredith swung the shovel downward. The blade caught the corner of his ear and cut into his flesh.

"Agh!" he screeched, stumbling forward.

She raised the shovel and struck again.

He dropped to his knees then crashed to the floor. The plate slammed against the cement, shattering.

Run! She stepped over his sprawled body. The harsh glare of the overhead light blinded her. Hesitating for an instant, she gathered courage to climb the stairs and face Hank, who still barred her escape.

Behind her Javier moaned.

No time to delay.

Meredith raced to the stairs.

Something touched her shoulder.

She turned, hands fisted, ready to strike.

"Pete?"

THIRTEEN

Black hair tumbling around her shoulders, Meredith let out a yelp of surprise. The shock Pete initially saw on her face was replaced with relief as she stepped toward him.

He pulled her into his arms. His heart crashed against his chest with joy as he felt the softness of her skin and inhaled her womanly scent. He pulled her even closer, his lips caressing her hair.

"Oh, Pete," she moaned.

"It's okay, honey. I'll get you out of here."

She dropped her head onto his shoulder.

He wanted to hold her forever. Gratitude filled him. *Thank God he'd found her.*

But she was still in danger. They needed to get to the Jeep and head for safety.

Pulling her back, Pete stared into her eyes. "We've got to hurry."

She nodded and slipped her hand into his.

Fingers entwined, he was stirred by the sense of completeness he felt whenever they were together. Connected at last, he guided her behind the stairwell and tapped the palm of his free hand along the wall until a section pushed open, exposing the narrow tunnel cut into earth.

"I'll lead and you follow," he said.

Meredith pulled her hand back. "I…I can't."

He drew the Maglite from his pocket and played it over the walls. "It's safe. There's a little moisture from the rain, but the walls seem stable. We don't have far to go. The tunnel leads out back."

She shook her head, her eyes wide. "Don't ask me to go in there." She pointed to the second floor. "Hank's the only guy upstairs. He's Javier's partner. You can take him."

"He may have a gun, Meredith." With the rickety basement steps and Meredith's unbalanced gait, a surprise attack would be unlikely.

"I'll go first." Pete stepped toward the opening.

Something rustled behind them. They glanced in the direction of the sound.

Rubbing his head, the Latino stumbled from the darkness. He stopped abruptly.

Pete grabbed Meredith's arm.

She struggled to break free. "You don't understand. My adoptive father—"

Pete remembered the closet and pantry.

"He locked you up, didn't he?" If Pete ever came face-to-face with Collins, he'd smash him to a pulp. "Don't let him win, Meredith."

"I...I can't." She shook her head, refusing to budge.

"Hank," Javier yelled. "We got trouble."

Pulling his .45 from his waistband, he fired, hitting the wall next to Pete.

The overhead door opened, and footsteps sounded on the stairs.

"Come on, honey."

Meredith's eyes were wide with fear, but she didn't move. Pete lifted her into his arms.

Hank fired from the stairwell.

Holding Meredith close to his heart, Pete raced into the tunnel.

"No!" she screamed, hiding her face in the small of his neck.

A third shot exploded into the beam that shored up the earthen walls. The sound reverberated through the passageway.

Meredith whimpered.

"We're almost there," Pete mumbled. Shining the light ahead, he knew the men were right behind them. Even if they made it to the end of the tunnel, the two goons would overtake them outside.

A rumble sounded, then picked up momentum.

Dust billowed around them.

The roar grew louder.

Pete glanced over his shoulder. His heart crashed against his chest.

The earthen walls were imploding, like a chain reaction of falling dominoes.

He pushed on, seeing the opening dead ahead. He had to save Meredith.

Ten feet, eight…

Fissures on the sides of the tunnel grew wider, whole sections caving in.

Four feet to freedom. The air too thick to breathe.

Holding Meredith with one arm, Pete reached out with the other to where he'd seen the ladder only seconds ago. Now he could see nothing.

His fingers wrapped around the wooden rungs. He started to climb.

The earth groaned and, in one last shudder, crashed down around them.

His muscles strained, his lungs cried for air. He summoned every bit of strength to move forward and upward.

The top half of his body broke through the trapdoor. He hoisted Meredith onto the floor of the tiny shelter.

The earth caught his feet and sucked him down like quicksand. With one final surge, he pulled free and crawled onto the floor next to Meredith.

Gasping, he inhaled the sweet night air.

Pete touched her arm, feeling something warm and sticky.

He aimed the light.

Blood.

Darkness surrounded her. Meredith gasped for air, then coughed repeatedly to clear the dirt she'd inhaled in the tunnel.

"Are you okay?"

Pete's voice. She blinked her eyes open and saw his face close to hers.

"I didn't think I'd see those eyes again," he said.

"I'm…okay." She rolled onto her side and tried to rise, then moaned and fell back to the floor.

"Easy does it. A bullet grazed your arm."

Pete put his hand under her shoulders and helped her sit up.

"My Jeep's stashed in the woods. We need to get out of here."

With Pete's help, she managed to stand.

The world shifted. She collapsed against him, feeling his strength as he held her close.

"I'll carry you."

"No." She shook her head. "Give me a second. I can walk."

"We don't have time." Once again, he lifted her into his arms, careful not to jostle her injured arm.

Stepping through the doorway, he glanced back at the farmhouse.

She followed his gaze. "Where are Javier and Hank?"

The sound of an engine revved into life.

Headlights illuminated the clearing behind the house.

"In the truck headed this way," he said.

Her heart raced. Fear swept through her.

Pete carried her along the back edge of the clearing. For an instant, the headlights caught them in their glare. He turned onto a narrow path that wound through the undergrowth.

"They must have seen us," she said, hearing the quiver in her own voice.

Head against his chest, Meredith felt Pete's pounding heart. She clutched his shoulder, grateful for this caring man who put her needs before his own. If only she weren't such a burden.

With every step he took, pain seared her arm.

Her baby? *Oh, dear Lord, protect this child.*

Pete pushed on, his breathing labored. Branches scraped against them. He angled his body, protecting her from the dense underbrush that pulled at his clothes and slapped against his arms.

A thorny limb sliced across her leg. She held back a moan. Pete was doing so much to save her.

Meredith glanced over his shoulder.

Hank and Javier followed close behind them in the pickup. Their headlights flickered through the brush.

A shot sounded.

Pete stopped short. She turned and saw the Jeep.

In one swift movement, he threw open the door and laid her in the front seat. "Get down," he warned.

Slamming the door, he raced to the driver's side and slipped behind the wheel, key in hand.

Please, God, she prayed again.

A bullet pinged off the front bumper.

Pete turned the key and stepped on the gas.

The groan of an engine sounded behind them.

Meredith raised her head and glanced out the window. The pickup had caught in the clutches of a fallen tree.

The doors swung open. Javier and Hank jumped to the ground, guns in hand.

The wheels of the Jeep spun in the soft, wet earth. Pete eased up on the accelerator. The tires grabbed and pulled free.

They moved forward, out of the glare of the pickup's headlights.

Meredith wrapped her good arm around her belly, feeling every bump in the path.

The road dipped. Her stomach roiled. "Oh," she cried, unable to help herself.

With a jolt, the Jeep climbed onto the pavement.

"We're clear," Pete said. He increased their speed, the road under them smooth.

Meredith let out a sign.

An intersection loomed ahead.

Sirens sounded in the distance.

Police!

She grabbed his arm. "Don't let them find me."

"Meredith, you need help."

"Not the police." They hadn't believed her when she was a child, when she had reported her adoptive father's abuse of her mother. They wouldn't believe her now.

The sirens neared, heading straight toward them.

"Please," she begged.

Pete hung a sharp left. The tires screamed in protest.

He hit the gas. Rubber burned as the Jeep lurched

forward, putting distance between them and the squad car.

"We need to talk," was all he said. His hands gripped the wheel, eyes trained on the road.

She'd have to tell him.

But not now.

Her wounded arm lay on her lap, the coppery smell of blood reaching her nose.

A dark spot soaked her shirt.

Raising her good arm, she rubbed her fingers over her stomach.

How long had it been since she'd felt movement?

Everything she cared about had been taken from her.

Not my baby.

Oh, dear God, not my baby, too!

FOURTEEN

Pete drove west, staying on the deserted roads and isolated stretches where few other cars traveled.

At least the night had cleared. He could see the North Star and the Big Dipper and knew they were headed away from the farmhouse and the maniacs who had captured Meredith. And away from the police she feared.

He glanced at her. He'd been so focused on the immediate danger that he hadn't noticed the tears that glistened on her cheeks.

The sense of relief he had felt shattered. He wanted to pull her into his arms and hold her close. But they had to keep moving.

He rubbed his hand across her arm.

She cringed at his touch. He raised his fingers into the light from the dash.

Blood.

His gut tightened.

Getting away from the police had been his primary concern. He hadn't realized the severity of her injury.

"How much blood have you lost?

"It's just a flesh wound," she mumbled.

Why did she always try to be so strong?

"Did you ever consider telling me the truth? You can trust me."

"I'm okay, really."

But he knew she wasn't. Glancing down at her lap, he saw the wet mark that darkened her blouse.

Anger welled up within him. At the men who had done this to her. But even more at himself for ignoring her need for first aid.

Above all else, he had wanted to protect her from the men in the farmhouse, and he had succeeded. Now another danger threatened her.

Where could he pull off the road to tend to her wound?

Pete turned onto an unpaved path and stopped behind a dilapidated, abandoned cabin that would shield them from anyone driving along the main road.

"What are you doing?" she asked, rising in the seat. A moan escaped her lips, and she fell back against the headrest.

Oh, yeah, she was in a lot of pain. Not that she'd readily share that information with him. She didn't share much of anything…not the reason her husband had been killed or what had happened in her past that caused her to be so fearful of the police.

"We're stopping so I can check your wound. I'll get the first aid kit in the back. Stay put."

He climbed out, unlatched the back door and grabbed the kit. The basic supplies would provide immediate triage for her wound.

Rounding to her side of the Jeep, he opened the passenger-side door. The overhead light snapped on.

Pete sucked air through his teeth.

Nothing superficial about this wound.

The bullet had cut a hole deep into her flesh.

He clamped down on his jaw. After he got Meredith to safety, he'd track down the thugs who had done this to her, wherever they tried to hide. If it were the last thing he did, he'd make sure they paid for hurting Meredith.

Those men needed to be knocked against a brick wall and pummeled until they couldn't walk.

Not that Pete believed in violence. But logical consequences were another thing entirely.

Pulling the Maglite from his pocket, Pete loosened the barrel until the powerful beam played over her wound.

Meredith glanced down and gasped.

"It's okay, honey," he assured her.

But it wasn't okay. Loss of blood and infection were the two biggest worries.

He grabbed a vial of Betadine to clean the wound. "This might hurt."

He poured the antiseptic solution over the wound. Her good hand clutched the armrest, but she didn't make a sound.

His heart went out to her. She was one strong woman.

"I'm sorry," he whispered.

Ripping open a sterile gauze packet, he dabbed the four-by-four square against the wound, cleaning out the dirt and debris that clung to the raw flesh.

She turned her head away, clutching the armrest even tighter.

"Almost done."

His probes opened the wound more, and a new flow of bright red blood poured forth.

Not what she needed or he wanted.

Pete passed over the latex tourniquet used for drawing blood and pulled an ACE bandage from the kit instead. Ripping open the plastic covering, he wrapped the stretchy gauze around her upper arm and pulled it tight.

She moaned. The sound cut right through him.

He hated causing her more pain, but the flow of blood had to be stopped.

At least the gauze would be more comfortable long-term than the narrow strip of latex.

Grabbing more four-by-fours, he squirted a gob of antibiotic ointment over the squares, then positioned them on the wound and taped the gauze in place.

If only the ointment was strong enough to retard the growth of bacteria. She didn't need an infection on top of everything else.

What she needed was medical care. Although the police would have to be notified. Not what Meredith wanted.

"I'll find the nearest hospital," he said when he slipped behind the wheel again and picked up his BlackBerry to do a map search, relieved to see the cell power up.

Surely even in this forsaken part of Georgia there had to be a medical facility.

If only he could get her there in time.

Meredith was worried, not so much about the wound but about the baby.

Pete was right. She needed to get to a hospital where a doctor could examine her.

When was the last time she'd felt the baby move?

At least Pete had rescued her from the farmhouse basement. Gratitude swelled within her, along with a growing awareness of his goodness and her own desire to stay with him. She glanced his way.

Focused on the road, his brow was drawn tight. His eyes searched the night, as if willing a hospital to materialize in the darkness.

"Any idea where we are?" she asked.

He glanced her way. "South of Augusta and east of Atlanta."

Having grown up in Augusta, Meredith said, "The Medical College of Georgia and its affiliated hospital are in Augusta."

"I'm hoping we can find something closer. The map search listed a community hospital not far from here."

She looked down at her arm. "The bleeding stopped."

"Good. What about the baby?"

"No movement."

"A change of position might help," he suggested.

"Whenever I sew, I bend over the fabric and usually get a solid kick in the side."

Pete tilted his head. "Want to give it a try?"

He helped her slide forward in the seat. The movement sent pain screaming down her arm.

She held her breath until the pain eased.

"You okay?" His eyes flicked back and forth from the road to her.

"Yeah. Just a reminder that I've got a hole in my arm."

"Check the blood flow." He turned on the interior light for a moment.

She examined the bandage. "It's okay."

The headlights cut through the night as they continued to drive along the back roads.

Meredith placed her good elbow on her knee and rested her head on her hand, putting pressure on her stomach. Hopefully, it wouldn't further distress the tiny life growing within her.

Right now, she needed some sign that the baby was all right.

"Mind if I sing?"

Pete looked at her, brow raised.

"I make up lullabies while I work. They seem to soothe the little one."

He had to smile. "You want the baby to move, Meredith. Not sleep."

"Yes, but usually I get an initial kick, as if she— or he—likes my singing."

"It's worth a try."

She sang about a mother's love and how she'd never let anything happen to her baby.

Tonight, the words caught in her throat. Tears

filled her eyes, and she blinked to clear them, then swiped her hand over her face as they broke free and rolled down her cheeks.

Hopefully, Pete wouldn't see her show of emotion. He'd done so much for her, and she could feel the concern in his gaze.

"I'm not sure this will work," she finally said with a sniff.

"The song was nice. Kind of got to me, if you know what I mean."

Yeah, she did know. Neither of them had known their mothers, which was hard for a child. And while Pete's dad hadn't been abusive, per se, he had made Pete's childhood less than the nurturing time it should have been.

Her voice was low, her tone guarded when she finally asked, "Were you ever locked away?"

He reached for her hand. His face was torn with anguish. "I'm sorry about what Collins did to you."

The warmth of his touch and the compassion she heard in his voice encouraged her. "The hardest part was when he'd come home with a surprise. Maybe chocolate candy or a carton of ice cream. For a few minutes I'd think everything would be okay. That we could be a happy family."

"You'd let your guard down."

She nodded. "And then he'd grab me and throw

me into the closet or the cellar or the shed out back and the darkness would seem even blacker, even more evil."

"He was a twisted man, Meredith. How'd you get the courage to run away?"

She had never told anyone, not even Ben. But tonight, after everything that had happened, she knew she could trust Pete.

"My adoptive mother gave me a Bible, but she told me to hide it so he wouldn't find it. Before I'd go to sleep, I'd read a few verses, usually not even understanding what the words meant. But I knew God loved me." She paused. "Sounds funny, I know, yet I had a feeling someone was praying for me."

He turned and nodded. "Eve was. She said she never stopped praying for you."

Meredith prayed constantly for the life growing within her. If what Pete said was true, maybe Eve *had* loved her. Meredith needed to believe that.

Although right now she wasn't ready to accept that love.

"You finally ran away." Pete drew her back into the conversation.

"He beat my mother. But never where it showed. People couldn't see the bruises on her stomach or across her thighs. I went to the police once. They called my father, who said I was an unruly child. He claimed I often hit my mother. He had her lower her dress to expose an ugly mark on her back that he said I had caused."

She looked out the window into the darkness, remembering the darkness of that night. "They believed him."

"And your mother?"

"She didn't say anything. She couldn't. He used to fool around with tracking devices so he always knew where she was. We both understood that if she'd spoken against him to the authorities, he would have killed her. Only we didn't realize that he would eventually do just that."

"What happened?"

"He pushed her down the basement steps. She hit her head, blood spewed everywhere. I was in the kitchen, washing the dishes. He turned and railed against me, screaming that I had pushed her, that I'd pay for causing her death."

Meredith licked her lips. "When he scrambled down the steps to check on her, I ran from the house. It happened right before my graduation from high school when I planned to leave him. In the woods, I had hidden some clothes and a little money my mother occasionally gave me from her shopping allowance. That night I left Augusta and hitched a ride out of town. My husband saw me on the road and gave me a ride."

"You fell in love with the man who rescued you."

"I'm not sure how much was love and how much was the need for security. Ben took me to the home of a nice Christian couple who had a spare room. I babysat their children and helped out around the house. Eventually, Ben and I got married."

"Did you ever hear from Collins again?"

She shook her head. "I knew he might be able to find me through my cell phone with all the tracking gadgets he bought online. Eventually, I realized he was probably relieved not to have me underfoot."

"And your husband's death?"

"Ben got a loan against his paycheck from some unscrupulous characters right before the plant where he worked closed. We couldn't make the payments. The loan shark Javier and Hank worked for wanted to make an example of Ben."

"So they offered him a job on a fishing boat and killed him at sea?"

"And threatened me after Ben's death not to tell the police about the loan. I ran and ended up in Refuge Bay. The next time I saw these thugs was when they parked outside my house."

"Dixie Collins was at your cottage the day before

we met. Ever think this might have less to do with the loan and more to do with you?"

Before Meredith could make sense of what Pete had just said, he pointed to a road sign. "Look what we found."

She followed his gaze and spied the sign with a large *H* painted in the middle of a square of blue.

Once again, she rubbed her belly. *Hold on, little one. Won't be long and we'll be at the hospital.*

Glancing at the clock on the dash, she asked, "Mind turning on the radio for the news? Maybe we can get an update on Sheila's condition."

Pete pushed the control knob. Static filled the car, then an announcer's voice. "Peace talks continue in the Middle East between Israel and Palestine."

Meredith sighed. "Reminds me of some of the family fights my adoptive mother used to talk about."

"Ever hear of the Hatfields and McCoys? Their feud was legendary."

"Weren't they from the hills of East Tennessee?"

"That's right. The McCoy side of the family suffered from VHL."

"You're kidding?"

He shrugged. "Intermarriage was common, which perpetuated the disease. Some say their medical problems added to the animosity they harbored for the Hatfields."

"Where's Eve from?"

Pete laughed. "Not Tennessee. Still, it's interesting to see how VHL can affect a family. I told you adrenal tumors can cause problems during childbirth, which we'll mention to the doctor when we get to the hospital."

A country-western song came on the radio. Pete hit the scanner.

The lights of the hospital shone in the distance. The two-story structure sat on a rise and looked out over a tiny valley. A town lay nestled in the distance.

Relief swept through Meredith. She and the baby would get medical help. Exactly what they both needed.

Please, God, she pleaded. *Keep this baby safe.*

As they neared the medical facility, her euphoria plummeted. Two police cars were parked side by side under a streetlight at the rear of the parking lot.

Pete decelerated to turn onto the access road for the E.R. just as a news flash came over the radio.

"Now an update on Sheila Hudson. The VHL Institute founder remains in critical condition, although she was able to provide some information to the police. An all-points bulletin has been issued for Peter Worth, thought to be traveling with his girlfriend, who answers to the name of Meredith. According to a 911 tip, the pair had holed up at a farmhouse in the vicinity of Old Buckhead Church and are considered armed and dangerous. The woman is pregnant and may be injured. Police are narrowing their search around Jenkins County and hospitals in the area."

Pete clicked off the radio. "I bet Javier and Hank called 911 to take the heat off themselves."

Meredith pointed to the sedans. "If they think we attacked Sheila, they'll throw us in jail and ask questions later. Keep driving, Pete."

He shook his head. "You need a doctor."

"But they'll lock me up."

He stared at her, then sighed in frustration. "Get down."

She doubled over as best she could in the seat.

Pete focused on the rearview mirror. "The cops turned on their lights."

Her heart pounded hard against her chest. She couldn't—wouldn't—let her baby be born in prison.

Plus, Sam Collins had vowed to make her pay for his wife's death. He had contacts with the police in Augusta, which wasn't far from here. For all she knew, the men in the squad cars could be friends of his as well.

A lone siren pierced the silence, then a second joined in, both wailing in the night.

Pete pulled the Jeep to the side of the road.

A lump formed in Meredith's throat. She had wanted everything to be perfect for this baby.

How had her life gotten so far off track?

Despite her faith in God, even He seemed to have abandoned her.

"I'm sorry, Meredith." Pete touched her hand. His fingers wove through hers. He looked down at her, his gaze filled with tenderness and compassion.

Her heart swelled, and peace settled over her.

She wasn't alone. God had sent Pete to help her in her time of need.

Meredith squeezed his hand. Good had come from all the bad. At least at this moment, she was connected to a strong, supportive man. A man of virtue and integrity. A man she was growing to love.

The sirens screamed, drawing closer. Lights pulsated, catching them in their glare.

Would everything end in the next few seconds or would God help them yet again?

"Thy will be done," Meredith whispered from the core of her being. The emptiness she'd felt for so long was filled with her love for Pete, as if the Lord Himself had wrapped them together in His Fatherly embrace.

She had placed her trust in God, and He had

answered her prayers. The Almighty had given her Pete to love and care for her and her unborn child.

The squad cars neared, the sound deafening, the lights blinding.

She held her breath, not knowing what would happen next.

At that moment, the baby kicked.

FIFTEEN

Pete let out the breath he'd been holding as the police cruisers raced past them, heading toward the lights of the town, visible in the distance. Seconds later, an ambulance followed in pursuit.

Meredith slumped back against the seat.

"Close call," Pete mumbled. He squeezed her hand, hoping to reassure her that they were out of danger.

Meredith's face had drained of color. Her eyes were closed, lips moving. Was she offering up a prayer of thanksgiving?

"Say one for me."

She opened her eyes and smiled. "I've got us both covered."

Pete ached to hold her.

Before he knew what he was doing, he drew her into his arms, being careful to avoid her wound. Her hair spilled around his face like satin.

She pulled back ever so slightly and stared into his eyes.

The world stopped for him at that moment.

"Pete." She sighed.

He lowered his mouth to hers.

Before their lips met, a car door slammed and someone cried for help.

An elderly man stumbled toward the entrance of the E.R. Two nurses rushed to his aid. They quickly settled him into a wheelchair and pushed him through the automatic doors.

Meredith straightened in the seat.

Pete wove his fingers through her hair and leaned close. "You still need to see a doctor," he whispered, his voice thick with emotion.

She shook her head. "Not here."

"But the baby?"

"I felt movement. The baby kicked just as the police passed by. It's a sign that everything's okay."

He grabbed the stethoscope off the back seat and wrapped it around his neck. "At least humor me."

Placing the base of the stethoscope against her stomach, he heard a strong heartbeat.

"Baby seems to be okay."

An I-told-you-so smile crept across her face. "Got any ideas where two fugitives can hide out?"

As much as he didn't want this moment to end,

he knew they needed to keep moving. A destination came to mind, but he wasn't sure Meredith would approve. "Let me handle our itinerary. Okay?"

"More back roads?"

"Roger that. We'd make better time on the highway, but I'm afraid we might be spotted."

He pulled away from the curb and turned onto a narrow two-lane road that headed west.

Meredith settled back against the seat. She closed her eyes and before long her breathing slipped into the even rhythm of sleep.

Just what she needed.

Pete couldn't help but glance at her, taking in the curve of her lips and the way her hair curled over her shoulder. He wanted to pull her back into his arms.

Meredith was a special lady. Her strength and determination reminded him of Eve's.

He cared deeply for both women, and his heart went out to them. If his plan worked, he'd be able to bring mother and daughter together.

Hopefully, a higher power would take it from there.

Now he was thinking about God?

He shook his head and smiled. Meredith must be having an effect on him. Or maybe his change of heart was due to Eve's prayers. She loved Meredith, and she claimed to love him as well.

In the depth of his soul, he knew that was true. He'd been the one to turn his back on Eve.

When he heard her parents say that Pete Worth would amount to nothing of worth, he'd felt not only anger at their play on his last name but also a massive blow to his pride.

He was young, and their degrading use of his name had cut him to the core. Succumbing to the hateful rhetoric his father spouted, Pete had turned on both the wealthy Townsends and Eve.

Now he needed her help.

The tires hit a rut in the road, and Meredith's eyes fluttered open. "Have you decided where we're going?"

She needed to know the truth.

"Atlanta. We can hole up at Eve's estate until everything dies down." Bad choice of words.

Meredith shook her head. "I told you I don't want to see her."

"It's either her estate or the police."

She glared at him. He'd pushed her into a corner. Not what he wanted to do, but he didn't have a choice. The police suspected them of trying to kill Sheila. Much as he didn't want to think about that possibility, if Sheila died, he and Meredith would be wanted for murder.

Eve had connections. While Pete didn't care for

Dr. Davis's VHL protocol, Eve might be able to convince him to treat Meredith's wound and check on the baby without notifying the authorities.

The lawyers Eve used were the best in the state, and she had the money to pay for their expertise. After everything that had happened, Pete and Meredith needed legal advice, too.

But as much as Eve had wanted to help Pete just two days ago, he wasn't sure she would open her heart or her home to him now.

Then he thought of the woman who'd held her arms wide so he could run to her as a child.

The old Eve wouldn't let him down.

Meredith turned toward the window. Hopefully, she'd mull over the situation and accept the only solution left to them.

She needed Eve—and her help.

Meredith didn't want to see her mother. Not now. Not when she was tired and injured and so very vulnerable.

Years ago, she'd believed her mother hadn't wanted her, hadn't loved her. Once Meredith had steeled herself to that reality, the pain of abandonment and loss she'd suffered for so long had eased. Probably because by then she'd built a protective wall around her heart, vowing never to open herself to the pain again.

That's why she'd married Ben, wasn't it? He had been a safe choice, never demanding more from her than she was willing to give.

Oh, God, forgive me for being so protective of my own feelings that I didn't think of his. My love was incomplete and surely that must have caused him pain.

Tears once again welled up in her eyes. After all these years of guarding her heart, the wall of isolation she'd built had started to crumble.

Pete stirred in the seat next to her.

He'd come to her rescue, ignoring his own safety to protect her and her child. His selfless concern for them evoked a depth of emotion she'd never before experienced.

Knowing the strength of her feelings for Pete only underscored how different her love for her husband had been. Now Pete wanted her to meet her mother.

Meredith could accept Pete into her life, but she wasn't ready to accept her mother's help.

"Isn't there someplace else we could go, other than the estate?" she begged.

"You need medical help, Meredith. Eve's family doctor treated her parents at the estate. I'm sure she'll convince him to help you as well. In a day or two, we'll go to the police and tell them the truth. By then, Sheila will have improved."

Meredith glanced away, unable to look at Pete with his sincere eyes and his voice of reason.

What if Sheila didn't make it?

Meredith shook her head, not wanting to think about that possibility.

If only life could be the way she'd planned. Instead, it was twisted and confusing, and Pete was forcing her to face a past she wanted to keep buried. Seeing Eve would open up too many wounds.

She glanced down at her arm.

Fresh blood stained the gauze.

Right now, she needed to rest. She would ask Pete to check her arm after she closed her eyes for a few minutes.

Hopefully, he'd know what to do because at this moment she wasn't sure of anything.

The night hung before them. Once again, Pete weighed their options. He knew Meredith didn't want to see Eve, but there wasn't any other place to go.

He continued to head west along the back roads, skirting the main highways. He hoped that this winding route to Atlanta would keep them clear of the law.

Luckily, Meredith had drifted back to sleep. Truth be told, he could use some rest as well, but only after he had her safely at the estate.

They weren't far. He needed to call Eve to prepare her.

He reached for his BlackBerry and punched in her number, knowing the middle of the night was a bad time for surprises.

SIXTEEN

The phone started to go to voice mail before Eve picked up.

"Hello?" She sounded tired and confused. Maybe a bit anxious about having a call in the middle of the night.

"It's Pete."

"Pete?" She breathed out his name. "Where are you?"

"Not far from Atlanta. You probably heard the news reports about Sheila. I didn't do it."

"I know."

He glanced at Meredith sleeping on the seat next to him. "I need a place to stay for a few days. Until everything blows over."

"And if it doesn't?"

"Then I'll ask for more help."

"Fair enough. The servants start work at 8:00 a.m. I'll call and give them some time off."

"Thanks. Meredith's with me. She's been hurt. Could you contact Dr. Davis and see if he's willing to make a house call? But only if he can be trusted."

"I thought you didn't approve of him."

Pete pulled in a deep breath. "Seems I've been wrong about a lot of things."

"And what caused your change of heart?"

He hesitated, searching for words to explain how he felt. "I asked God to help me find Meredith, and He did."

"You sound surprised. I take it you still have problems accepting Him into your life."

Pete stared into the darkness ahead, trying to find his way. "It's the part about miracles, Eve. If He has the power to change lives, why doesn't He help you?"

"Suffering makes us stronger. Remember Christ suffered and died on the cross for our sins."

"There's nothing redeeming about VHL."

"But because of my illness, I decided to find my daughter."

"You would have come to that same conclusion without going through all the pain."

"Perhaps. But what about you? Your mother died in childbirth. Your father did more to hide his love than show it. I know it hurt you to leave the estate."

"Evidently, your parents didn't feel the same way." She sighed. "Your father never told you, did he?"

"About *your* father's plan to cut costs by doing away with the groundskeeper position. Three years and my dad would have earned his pension."

"Is that how your dad explained the problem?"

"Meaning what, Eve?"

"Meaning he didn't tell you the whole story. About inflated expense reports for the upkeep of the property. Money your father stole from the estate."

Pete bristled. "I don't believe you."

"Did you really think my folks would fire your dad just to keep from paying him his retirement? Besides, he continued to receive a sizable monthly stipend. Something I insisted on. In addition to the extra money I gave him for you."

Pete held the phone to his ear while his eyes focused on the road…on the beam of headlights sweeping across the asphalt…on anything except what Eve was saying.

"I didn't tell you about the money he stole from the estate because you needed to hear it from your own father, not from me. Time's running out for me, Pete. I'm trying to right wrongs from the past and reconnect with the people who are important to me. You're at the top of the list."

Emotion clogged his throat.

"The past is over. Come home, Pete. I'll be waiting for you just as I have been for so long."

He heard firm resolution in her voice but also tenderness and acceptance.

"I love you as if you were my flesh and blood," she continued. "You're a wonderful man with a good sense of right and wrong. God loves you, too. Just open the door to your heart."

He could open the door for Eve, but he still had reservations about God.

"Think about it and we'll talk more when you get to the estate."

Disconnecting, Pete dropped the BlackBerry onto the console.

His eyes fell on Meredith. Her arm lay draped around her stomach.

A new spot darkened her blouse and slacks.

"Meredith?" He nudged her shoulder. "Wake up, honey."

She failed to respond.

Meredith heard Pete call her name, but the hum of the tires and the lull of the engine soothed her back into a deep slumber. She was somewhere bright and beautiful, holding her baby.

The car stopped and a door slammed. She tried to open her eyes, but the effort proved too difficult.

A hand touched hers.

She gasped with pain that shot up her arm and through her shoulder. A low moan escaped from her lips. She blinked, seeing Pete's face.

His brow was wrinkled with worry. "Hold on, Meredith."

He lifted her into his arms.

Her head found the cleft in his neck. She snuggled into him, hearing his heart pound, feeling the strength of his embrace.

They were hurrying up a stone walkway.

A mansion towered over them. Three stories rimmed with balconies. Tall white columns. Gaslights that greeted them from the porch.

Before Pete could knock, the massive door opened. A woman motioned them inside. Slender with upswept hair, her green eyes reflected the worry in Pete's.

Eve.

He said something. Meredith tried to focus on her response.

"Dr. Davis will be here shortly. He wants you to draw Meredith's blood and do a workup at Magnolia Medical. He mentioned a CBC and chemistry profile."

"I picked up a phlebotomy kit at the Institute. It's in the car."

Eve ushered them down a long hallway and into a room just off what appeared to be a huge study. "We'll keep her comfortable until Dr. Davis arrives. He should be here shortly."

"Davis won't call the cops?"

"He'll talk to you before he makes that decision."

Pete laid Meredith on the thick comforter. The room swirled around her in a mix of deep blues and magenta. She sank into the softness of the bedding.

He elevated her injured arm on a pile of pillows and repositioned the tourniquet.

"The bleeding's stopped. At least for now."

Stepping toward the bed, Eve held a quilt pieced with small hearts and tiny crosses.

The same pattern as the baby coverlet Meredith had been wrapped in when her real mother gave her up for adoption.

Eve covered her with the thick quilt, then brushed her cool hand lovingly over Meredith's brow.

A lump clogged Meredith's throat. Hot tears stung her eyes. Tears of joy.

Pete had brought her home.

Home to her mother.

Returning to her bedside, he drew vials of blood from the vein in her uninjured arm. She saw him as if through a fog.

Closing her eyes, she sensed her body drift into a better place. Before she left Pete, she dropped her good hand to her stomach and caressed her child one last time.

SEVENTEEN

Pete turned into the Magnolia Medical lot and parked in a secluded spot behind the incinerator building, a small brick structure that sat away from the main facility. Hidden from the road and shadowed from the streetlights, his Jeep wouldn't attract attention while he completed Meredith's blood tests.

Using his passkey to enter through a side door, he climbed the stairs to the third floor. His footsteps echoed in the long hallway. Stopping in front of the entrance marked with the biohazard sign, he keyed the metal door open and stepped into the lab. The smell of chemicals hung in the air, along with a hint of bleach used to disinfect the work areas.

He shrugged into a lab coat and slipped latex gloves over his hands. Pete worked swiftly, concentrating on the tests Dr. Davis needed to assess Meredith's condition.

Placing a clean glass slide on the workbench, he made a smear of her blood and, once stained, placed it under the microscope. Settling into the tall stool, he adjusted the ocular and watched the kaleidoscope of cells swarm into view. An increased number of white blood cells signaled the beginning of a bacterial infection. A serious complication, but something else troubled him more.

The decreased number of red blood cells.

Automated analyzers spewed out additional test results. Pete pulled the lab slips from the machines. A sense of dread settled on his shoulders.

Worse than he had expected. The sophisticated instrumentation confirmed that Meredith had lost far too much blood.

Racing to the blood bank, Pete performed a rapid blood type. Meredith tested B positive. He pulled four units from the Jewett refrigerator and crossmatched them for transfusion. Placing the units in a biohazard transport box, he added an ice pack from the freezer and closed the lid.

Slipping the strap of the container over his shoulder, Pete grabbed the lab printouts and everything Davis would need to start the transfusion, then retraced his steps through the lab.

As he left the building, he called Eve.

"How's Meredith?"

"About the same. She keeps mumbling something about the quilt."

"When Davis arrives, tell him her hematocrit is low. I crossmatched four units of blood. He'll be able to start a transfusion as soon as I get there."

"I'm expecting him any minute."

Pete needed to get back to the estate ASAP. Davis would arrive shortly, and Pete wanted everything ready.

Meredith's life and the life of her baby depended on how quickly she received the blood.

Meredith heard the doorbell through the haze of sleep.

She opened her eyes to the beautiful room and the quilt that covered her. Running her fingers over the pieced fabric, she felt a sense of connection.

From the hallway, Eve's voice was raised.

What did she say?

A second voice sent goose bumps to pimple her flesh.

No!

She needed to warn Eve.

Pushing up on her good elbow, Meredith tried to rise from the bed. The effort sapped her energy, and she fell back onto the pillows.

Her eyes closed.

Voices echoed through her mind. Was she dreaming?

No reason to face something that was only a memory.

She'd have time to do that later. After her baby was born. After she said goodbye to Pete.

Regret tugged at her heart. She didn't want to leave Petc.

Acceptance and love was all she'd ever wanted, and that's what she'd found with him.

EIGHTEEN

Pete placed the insulated blood transport container on the floor of his Jeep behind the driver's seat. His neck tingled as footsteps sounded behind him. He turned and spied the two thugs from the farmhouse.

"You guys ever give up?"

Hank brandished a knife. He wiped his fingers over the sharp blade and sneered. "Not until we finish the job."

He lunged.

Pete sidestepped away from the car and clear of the knife.

Javier circled from the left.

Pete flicked his gaze back and forth, keeping both men in sight.

The Latino pulled the .45 from his waistband. As he fumbled with the slide to chamber the round,

Pete grabbed the gun and jammed his fist into the guy's gut. Air rushed from his lungs.

Pete struck again, and Javier fell to the ground.

Hank lashed out with the knife, catching Pete's flesh and ripping a gash in his left side. Blood seeped from the wound.

Pete aimed the gun. "Drop the knife and anything else you're packing."

Hank's eyes widened. "Hey, man, don't shoot." Hank yanked a revolver from his belt and tossed it away from him. The knife clattered to the pavement as he raised his hands over his head.

Pete kicked it aside with his foot. "Who are you working for?"

Hank lowered his gaze.

Pete grabbed his neck and shoved him against the car. His hand clamped down hard on the punk's throat. "You'd better start talking."

He shook his head, eyes wide with fear. "The guy's in jail. Before he was arrested, he made a deal with someone called Mule. He's been tracking you through your cell phone."

Pete loosened his hold. "Go on."

"Look, we've never seen him. Mule calls us, tells us what he wants and we do it."

"And exactly what *does* Mule want?"

"The woman."

An icy jolt of fear ran through Pete's veins. They'd tracked him to Magnolia Medical, thinking Meredith was with him. Luckily, she was safe at the estate.

"Grab your friend." Pete pointed to Javier still sprawled on the pavement.

Hank helped his partner to his feet.

Unlocking the door to the incinerator building, Pete shoved them inside and tied their hands behind their backs to the levers that turned on the giant gas oven.

"Wiggle around too much and you'll start the fire. Of course, you probably won't live to regret your mistake. My suggestion: you stay put. Someone will burn trash later today. I want them to find you alive."

Pete looked at the .45 in his hand. With sure swift moves, he released the magazine, then pulled back the slide and ejected the round from the chamber.

"Didn't your parents ever tell you not to play with guns?" He threw the weapon into the trash bin before he stepped outside, locking the door behind him.

Pulling his BlackBerry from his pocket, he tapped in Eve's number, relieved to hear her voice when she answered.

"I'm on my way. Don't let anyone in except the doc."

"Be careful, Pete."

He disconnected and glanced down. Blood seeped from his side.

Opening the back of the Jeep, Pete snatched an ACE bandage from his first aid kit. He raised his shirt, stuck a wad of four-by-fours against the cut and wrapped the stretchy bandage around his abdomen. A makeshift fix, but it would hold back the flow of blood.

Once Doc Davis treated Meredith, Pete would have him check his own wound.

Her condition would determine when they turned themselves in to the police. Until then, they needed some calm in the storm.

He looked down again. Blood had already soaked through the gauze.

Seemed everything kept getting darker.

NINETEEN

The floodlights that usually spotlighted the estate grounds were off when Pete pulled into the long driveway and approached the house where a lone porch light cut through the darkness.

A late-model Cadillac sat in front. Doc Davis's car, no doubt.

Grabbing the insulated blood container and the lab test results, Pete raced to the porch.

Davis opened the door, a pale, slender man, mid-fifties. He stepped aside as Pete rushed into the foyer.

"I've got the lab printouts. Meredith's lost a lot of blood. Her hematocrit is down. Electrolytes are out of whack, and her white blood count's elevated." Pete shoved the papers into the doctor's hands. "How's the baby?"

Davis shook his head. "I just got here."

Pete started down the hall, heading for the guest room. "Follow me, doc."

Davis grabbed his arm. "Eve wants to see you in the study first."

"What?"

"It's important."

Nothing was as important as Meredith and her child.

"I'll see what Eve wants. You check on Meredith." Pete placed the transport container on the side table. "I crossmatched four units. Everything you need is in the box."

"This way." Davis motioned for Pete to follow him through the formal living room that led to the study.

Pete clamped down on his jaw, irritated by the doc's attitude. Meredith needed medical attention. This wasn't the time to be playing host. "I know the way, doc."

"Pete, is that you?" Eve called to him, her voice strained.

No wonder. Harboring two fugitives on the run had to be affecting her. Not what she expected or wanted.

Not what Pete had wanted, either.

He stomped into the study ready to point Davis through the rear door that led to the back hallway and the guest room. Every minute was critical for Meredith.

But he quickly saw the problem.

Eve sat at her desk, her hands on the keyboard of her computer.

She looked up at him over the monitor. Brow furrowed, face drawn. Fear flashed from her eyes. "Peter, have you met Sam Collins?"

Big guy. Ponytail. The same man he'd seen with Dixie two nights ago now stood next to Eve, holding a gun to her head.

Pete stopped short. "Sa-muel. So you're Mule?"

"He's Dixie's father," Eve corrected.

Pete shook his head. "Dixie's not his daughter. She's his girlfriend."

"My dead girlfriend, to be exact."

"Was she too demanding? Is that why you murdered her, just like you murdered your wife?"

Collins sneered. "Meredith has a big mouth." He placed his free hand on Eve's neck. "I told Hank and Javier to take care of you."

Eve flinched, her eyes wide.

"Don't hurt her, Collins."

He glanced at the blood on Pete's shirt. "Appears the boys did a little damage."

"Yeah, but I'm the one left standing."

Collins grimaced. His hand continued to caress Eve's neck.

She tried to pull away.

He gripped her hair and yanked her head back. "I told you to hold still."

Time to calm things down a bit. Pete held up his hands. "Eve, it's okay. Do what he says."

He looked at Davis. The doc glanced down at the tall stone figurine sitting on the coffee table.

Pete got the message loud and clear.

Distract Collins and Davis would grab the statue. Divide and conquer. With a little luck, it might work.

Although with the gun jammed into Eve's temple, they needed more than luck.

"What's with the computer?" Pete asked, hoping to deflect Collins's attention.

He smiled, his puffy eyes narrowing into slits. "Eve's sending a little money to an overseas account I have."

"So that's what this is about. You want her money."

"Which I could have had if my plan to pass Dixie off as her daughter had worked out."

His hand returned to Eve's neck. "Only you needed a DNA specimen."

"My…my lawyers demanded it," Eve stammered, her voice thick.

"How'd you find Meredith?" Pete asked, buying time.

"Luck. A news article about her murdered husband ran a photo of the grieving widow." Collins chuckled. "Wasn't hard to locate the loan sharks working that area of coastal Georgia. Hank and Javier were working for a man who's now in jail. Stupid fools. They spooked her. But then you were there that night at her beach bungalow, spying on us. The only things I found were a few quilt squares and the bill for her cell phone."

"Once you had her cell number, you used a tracking device to keep tabs on her."

Collins nodded. "Amazing, the technology you can buy online."

"You told Javier and Hank we were at Sheila Hudson's home in Savannah. Meredith called a mechanic while we were there, which pinpointed our location. If you had a swatch of Meredith's hair, maybe even a blood specimen, you could submit them for DNA testing and claim they were from Dixie, proving she was Eve's daughter."

"Only you ruined my plans."

"Why make up a story about Dixie when Meredith was Eve's real daughter?"

Collins's eyes narrowed again, but this time he wasn't smiling. "As if she would have given me anything. She was ungrateful, even though I did everything for her."

"You locked her in the basement. In closets. Not the way most folks treat their children."

Eve gasped. She turned to face Collins, her hands clenched and poised to strike the man who had hurt her child.

The distraction was just what they needed.

Davis grabbed the statue. As he swung at Collins, Pete shoved Eve into the corner for safety.

The statue missed its mark and dropped to the floor.

Collins fired.

Davis grabbed his chest and fell backwards onto the couch. A gush of crimson spread across the plush velvet cushions.

"Don't move." Collins turned the gun on Pete, then motioned Eve back to the keyboard.

She shook her head and stood flush against the mahogany sideboard, her hands clutching the knob on the drawer. "I…I can't think straight."

Pete glanced at the monitor. Eve hadn't completed the transfer of funds.

Not wanting her near Collins, Pete stepped toward the computer. "I'll do it."

Pete looked at Eve. He nodded ever so slightly, trying to reassure her. "What's your password?"

"Your birth date, followed by your middle name. Lowercase, no spaces."

He tapped in the code. The file opened.

Checking the figures, he quickly realized that while the funds in the account were insignificant compared to Eve's total assets, Collins would be able to live comfortably for the rest of his life.

"You won't get away with this," Pete warned.

Collins chuckled. "I'll be in the islands before the police even know I'm out of the country. From there, I'll just keep going."

And kill all of us before you leave here, Pete thought.

He saw movement out of the corner of his eyes and turned ever so slightly.

Oh, dear God, no.

Meredith stood in the entryway, her good arm propped against the doorjamb for support.

"I won't let you hurt anyone else." Her voice was weak but filled with accusation.

Collins sneered. "My lovely daughter."

"Who ran away from you when you killed your wife," Pete said, once again hoping to distract him.

Out of the corner of his eye, Pete saw Eve open the top drawer and pull out the .32 caliber revolver she kept in the house for protection. She raised the revolver and fired. The bullet pinged against the fireplace.

Pete lunged for Collins's gun. It went off, grazing Pete's shoulder.

Ignoring the pain, he grabbed Collins's hand. They fought for control of the weapon.

Eve fired again. The bullet hit Collins's arm. Blood streaked his shirt.

Too close for comfort. "Hold your fire," Pete yelled.

He smashed his fist into Collins's gut. The guy hardly flinched.

Collins grabbed Pete's arm and twisted. Pain ricocheted through his body.

Pete broke free. Collins stooped to retrieve the gun, but Pete kicked it across the room.

Meredith slithered down the doorjamb, groping across the floor with her hand.

Hearing her moan, Pete turned. Collins caught him off guard with a jab to his injured left side.

Gasping, Pete doubled over.

Collins reached for the stone statue and raised it over his head.

Pete had to stop him.

He charged.

"No!" Eve screamed. She aimed the revolver.

Meredith's fingers wrapped around Collins's gun.

Collins swung the statue. Two shots exploded, ripping into his chest. Air rushed from his lungs.

The statue fell from his hands and shattered. Slowly and deliberately, Collins crumpled to the floor.

Pete raced to Meredith's side. She lay in a pool of blood and water.

He touched her cheek. "Meredith?"

Her eyes were closed, her face pale as death.

TWENTY

"Call 911!" Pete screamed to Eve. He knelt over Meredith and felt for a pulse. Weak. Too weak.

Eve fumbled with the phone, tapped in the digits and relayed the information when the operator answered. "Emergency. Send an ambulance."

"And the police," Pete prompted.

Meredith's skin was white as chalk. She'd lost so much blood.

Pete raced into the hallway and returned with the insulated container in hand.

Every army medic knew how to start an IV and administer meds and blood, which was what Meredith desperately needed.

He ripped open an alcohol swab, cleaned her arm and inserted the IV needle, relieved when he hit the vein on the first try.

Within minutes, he had the unit of blood dripping

life back into Meredith. Would it be enough to save her?

Please, God.

Eve knelt next to him on the floor, wiping her hand over Meredith's brow.

"Oh, Lord, save this precious child of mine," she prayed over and over again.

Sirens sounded in the distance. Pete opened the door and led the police and emergency personnel into the study, hastily explaining what had happened.

He pointed to Meredith. "She may have adrenal tumors that could increase her blood pressure during delivery. Her water broke. She might be in labor."

Meredith was the first to be placed on a stretcher and rolled to a waiting ambulance. Davis was hoisted into a second emergency van. Although critical, he was expected to live. Collins wasn't as lucky.

Eve crawled into the ambulance with Meredith and looked back expectantly for Pete.

"We need to talk to him," the officer in charge told her before the doors closed. Both ambulances drove off, their sirens wailing in the night.

Pete relayed the events of the last couple of days. The interrogation progressed rapidly, thanks to the lieutenant's grasp of the situation.

"From the looks of your injuries, maybe we should call another ambulance," the officer said when he had the information he needed. "The least we can do is give you a ride."

Pete accepted the offer. Grabbing Meredith's bag from his Jeep, he slipped into the back seat of the police sedan.

The flashing lights parted the traffic and moved Pete quickly to the E.R. entrance of Atlanta's large trauma center.

"She's been taken to L and D," the E.R. receptionist said, pointing him toward the elevators. "Looks like you need a doctor as well."

Pete ignored her comment, pushed the Up button on the elevator and got off at labor and delivery.

He found Eve in the waiting room, head resting in her hand. Pete touched her shoulder.

She looked up, her eyes red and rimmed with tears. "A nurse said she'd let me know. So far I haven't heard a thing."

Pete eyed the swinging double doors and the Do Not Enter sign, indicating the delivery area.

He stepped forward and pushed through the doors.

A nurse peered out from one of the labor rooms. "You can't come in here."

"Meredith Lassiter," he said. "Her mother's waiting outside. Any word on her condition?"

"We'll let you know when the baby's born."

"Keep close watch on her blood pressure. I told the EMTs, but they may not have passed the information on. Meredith could have Von-Hippel Lindau disease. Adrenal tumors would be a complication. Can you let her doctor know?"

The nurse nodded before she disappeared back into the labor room.

After reassuring Eve, Pete stepped into the men's room, startled by his own reflection in the mirror. Dark rings of fatigue circled his eyes. His brow was drawn, his face covered with dirt. A yellow bruise had started to form on his swollen cheek.

Forget his shirt and pants. Torn, bloodied, wrinkled. He needed a hot shower and some new clothes.

Instead, he splashed cold water on his face and washed up with the antiseptic soap from the wall dispenser.

The cleaned-up version didn't look much better.

His side ached and his arm could use a stitch or two.

All that would be handled later. Once Meredith was out of danger.

Returning to the waiting room, he sat next to Eve. "Any sign of the nurse?"

She shook her head. Her fingers fiddled with the

edge of her blouse. "I just found my daughter, thanks to you. I can't lose her now."

"She's a fighter, Eve."

"What about the baby?"

Two months ahead of schedule. Not the best situation, but Meredith was in the right place.

Surely, everything would work out.

Unless the adrenal tumor caused her blood pressure to spike. Had the nurse transmitted the information?

Maybe he should step back into the unit and talk with the doc one-on-one.

Pete rose as the swinging doors opened.

"Meredith Lassiter's family?" the nurse called.

Pete nodded, trying to read her expression.

"Meredith would like to see you." The nurse glanced at the bag sitting next to Pete's chair. "You can bring her things back."

He reached for the bag and helped Eve to her feet. They followed the nurse, not knowing what to expect.

"How is she?" Eve asked.

"You're her mother?"

"Yes, that's right." Eve stole a sideways glance at Pete.

"She's being transfused with a second unit of blood," the nurse explained as they walked. "The E.R. said she got one on the way to the hospital.

That raised her blood count. The doctor ordered two more units."

"And her blood pressure?" Pete asked.

"Actually, it's a little low."

Which meant adrenal tumors hadn't been a complication.

Pete let out the breath he'd been holding. "Thank the Lord."

Eve grabbed his hand and squeezed.

The nurse pointed them toward a room on the left of the corridor.

Pete held the door for Eve, then followed her in. Both of them stopped at the foot of the bed. Meredith's bandaged arm lay propped up on a pillow. The unit of life-giving blood slowly dripped into the vein in her other arm.

Her dark hair swarmed over the bed, contrasting sharply with her face, pale as the white sheets.

Her eyes were closed, and for a moment Pete feared the worst. Was she breathing?

"Meredith?" He stepped closer and touched her hand.

She opened her eyes. Her brow furrowed.

Did she recognize him?

"It's Pete," he prompted, then pointed to the foot of the bed. "Eve's with me. We wanted to see how you're feeling."

"Happy," she said, attempting to smile.

Joy coursed through him, pushing away the fear. "And the baby?"

"They're cleaning her up."

"Her?" Pete gripped her hand more tightly. "The baby's okay?"

"The doctor said I didn't have to worry about anything."

The door pushed open, and a different nurse rolled an incubator into the room. "Five pounds, two ounces and seventeen inches. Everything checked out fine. Seems you were closer to term than you thought."

She glanced at Pete's stained clothing and handed him a scrub gown. "Put that on if you hold the baby."

He slipped the protective covering over his shirt and pants.

The nurse picked up the swaddled baby and compared Meredith's armband to the tiny information tag around the infant's ankle. Satisfied that they matched, she placed the baby in Meredith's arms and left the room.

Pete gazed down at the most beautiful baby he'd ever seen. Tiny button nose, rosy cheeks and a bow of a mouth that trembled ever so slightly into a smile as if she were dreaming of something sweet.

"Oh, Meredith, she's perfect." Eve rubbed her hand over the baby's arm.

Noticing the bag Pete had placed near the rocking chair, Meredith said, "I've got a blanket in there. Would you pull it out?"

He unzipped her tote and found the quilted fabric folded at the bottom, recognizing the heart and cross pattern that matched the scraps he'd seen in her ocean bungalow just a few days before and also on the quilt Eve had covered Meredith with just hours earlier.

He handed the blanket to Meredith and smiled down at the healthy baby she'd just delivered. At this moment, it seemed as though they had always been a part of his life.

Eve touched the fabric. "It's the same cross-my-heart pattern I created for your baby quilt before you were born." She looked at Meredith, waiting for some explanation.

"Hazel Collins saved the quilt you made for me. When times were bad, I'd lay my head on the fabric, imagining I was laying my head on your lap."

Tears welled up in Eve's eyes. "I'm so sorry I gave you up for adoption. Especially to someone as terrible as Collins. When I think about how he treated you—"

Pete wrapped his arm around Eve and rubbed her shoulders.

Meredith reached for her hand.

"I'd do anything for my baby." Meredith looked down at the infant in her arms. "And I know you did what you thought was best for me."

"Sometimes things don't work out the way we plan," Eve whispered, her voice filled with emotion.

"Except they have. I wanted you in my life. Now you are and will be forever." Meredith looked into Eve's eyes, noting the brown mark that mirrored her own. "You'll always be in your granddaughter's life as well. If you don't mind, I'd like to name her Eve."

Meredith held the baby out to Grandma Eve, whose tears turned to joy as she took the tiny bundle into her arms. "Nothing could make me happier."

The glow of pride and love on her face said even more than her words. Eve carried the baby to the rocker, where she held her close and hummed the sweet strains of a lullaby.

Meredith reached for Pete's hand. "Thank you. You saved my life and my baby's life. You also reunited me with my mother."

"Everyone needs a family," he said.

"What about you, Pete?"

He raised his brow.

"Eve loves you dearly. It's evident every time she looks your way."

"I don't deserve her love."

"When I ran away from Collins, I had to accept the Lord's love into my life before I could begin to love myself. Only then could I love another."

"Your husband?"

"Pete, you're the one who has shown me the true meaning of love—sacrificial love. You placed my needs and the needs of my baby over your own. You're an honorable man of worth."

Pete stared down at her, this petite powerhouse of a woman who had been through so much. She'd been wounded and almost died. She'd fought off Collins and overcome the pain of her past to accept her mother's love.

So unassuming. So focused on others.

"I've never wanted anything as much in my life as to keep you and the baby safe."

She squeezed his hand. "I used to think I'd make a life for myself without having to rely on anyone else, but I learned that's not what I want now."

He stepped closer.

"Now, I know how important the love of another person can be."

Pete's heart swelled. He looked down at Meredith. He'd come full circle from the kid who had felt abandoned, just as Meredith had, to a man who had everything his heart desired…a woman to love, a new baby and a doting mother who cherished them all.

He thought of the disease that threatened Eve and could have been passed on to Meredith and her baby. Surely, the Lord would honor their prayers to give them more time together.

"We've only just begun to know each other," he said to Meredith. "But we've got a lifetime ahead of us."

"Yes," she whispered, drawing him close until their lips touched. At that moment, the baby cooed in Eve's arms.

EPILOGUE

The estate was aglow with tiny white lights, strung through the trees, and Japanese paper lanterns that danced in the breeze.

Pete stood on the patio and cradled baby Eve in his arms.

"It appears she likes you dressed up in a suit and tie." Grandma Eve laughed, causing the baby to giggle.

"She's feisty, like her mother." Pete cooed at the baby, then winked at Eve. "And her grandmother. How am I going to handle three women in my life?"

"Very nicely, I'm sure," Eve said.

Meredith stepped onto the patio. Her chiffon gown flowed around her, causing Pete to pull in a lungful of air and wonder if he were dreaming. She looked so beautiful. Her raven hair gleamed in the twinkling lights and her eyes danced with joy.

"Sorry, I'm late. I was explaining everything to the babysitter."

She grabbed Pete's hand. "Tell me you missed me."

He stooped to kiss her upturned mouth. "More than anything. But my other two girlfriends were keeping me company."

Meredith lingered over the kiss, then laughed as she playfully scooped baby Eve out of his hands, hugged the child tightly to her breast and then placed her in the babysitter's outstretched arms.

"Shall we go?" Eve asked. "The guests are waiting."

She led the way into the large tent where crystal chandeliers hung from the rafters. Silver candelabras and cloisonné vases filled with bouquets of fresh-cut flowers decorated the linen tablecloths, set with fine china and sterling flatware.

Over 150 guests, friends of Eve's and many of the most renowned names in the city, stood at their places as she and the guests of honor walked to the head of the table.

After a brief welcome, Eve asked Reverend Marks to offer the blessing.

"Heavenly Father, You have brought us to this joyous occasion to celebrate the goodness of Your abundant mercy. May we be strengthened by this food and enlivened by this gathering, and may the fellowship we enjoy tonight help open the doors of medical science so that all life may be fully lived. In Your holy name, O Lord, we pray."

"Amen."

As the minister returned to his place, Eve gazed at her guests. "Thank you all for being here for this special night to benefit VHL research. As you know, Pete Worth, who is like a son to me, is working on an important project in conjunction with the VHL Institute, which my dear friend Sheila Hudson founded."

Eve glanced at Sheila, who smiled and nodded to various people at the table.

"Working together with Magnolia Medical and the Institute can only bring further advances in VHL research as well as all cancers. Your donations tonight will make a lasting difference, and I thank you from the bottom of my heart." Smiling, Eve touched her hand to her heart. "Some of you know my most recent tests have shown improvement in my condition thanks to medical science and God's providence, which means I'll continue to serve as chair of the fundraising committee."

Her eyes fell on Meredith. "My daughter, who we were thrilled to learn does not carry the disease, has joined me in our effort to raise even more money for research. Thank you, dear."

Meredith smiled back at her mother.

"And now I'd like to make another very special announcement."

Pete wrapped his arm around Meredith. He looked down the table to where Veronica sat next to his graduate advisor.

"It is my pleasure—no, my joy—to announce the engagement of my daughter, Meredith, to Mr. Peter Worth, a man of honor and integrity and courage. A man who loves the Lord and who has committed his life to making the world a better place. I call him son. I'll soon be able to officially call him my son-in-law."

Eve raised her glass. "To Meredith and Pete. May the Lord bless them abundantly."

"Hear, hear," sounded around the table.

Pete wrapped Meredith in his arms and kissed her, thinking of the future they would share together.

Love, connection, family. What he had always wanted. What he had found with Meredith.

* * * * *

Dear Reader,

I first learned about Von Hippel-Lindau disease from my good friend Pat Rosenbach. She often talked about her friend Eva, who had VHL. Over the years, Eva underwent numerous surgeries to remove tumors that grew throughout her body. Eventually the tumors attacked her kidneys and became malignant.

Nine members of Eva's family have been diagnosed with VHL. Many of them participate in a study at the National Institutes of Health to aid scientists in developing treatments to combat this debilitating condition.

In hopes of helping others, Eva's sister Peggy Marshall started VHL Connections as a source of information and support for those who have the disease. To find out more about VHL, go to:

www.vhlconnections.org

or e-mail Peggy at:

vhlconnections@bellsouth.net

As I wrote this story, I tried to create characters that exemplify the courage and determination of so many who suffer from VHL. Truly, they are heroes. If you or someone you know has VHL, please tell them about VHL Connections.

I love to hear from my readers. E-mail me at Debby@debbygiusti.com or write to me c/o Steeple Hill, 233 Broadway, Suite 1001, New York, NY 10279. To learn about my next Love Inspired Suspense, visit me online at www.Debby-Giusti.com.

Wishing you abundant blessings,

Debby Giusti

QUESTIONS FOR DISCUSSION

1. Eve's parents forced her to give up her baby for adoption. Considering she was a young, unmarried teen, do you think her parents made a wise decision? What would you have done in their place?

2. Eve never married. Explain the reasons that may have played into her decision to remain single. Do you think she ever regretted not having a family?

3. What steps did Eve take to help Pete after he and his father left the estate? Could she have done more?

4. Why did Pete go into medical research? Do you think he realized the positive influence Eve had on his life?

5. As a child, Pete turned to Eve for love and support, but when he and his father were banished from the estate, he turned his back on

the woman who had been like a mother to him. How could their relationship have been saved?

6. When does Pete turn to God? How does the memory of finding his mother's cross help him seek the Lord?

7. When Pete learned the truth about his father, how did his relationship with Eve change?

8. In what way does the title, *Protecting Her Child,* refer to Meredith? Does it apply to Eve as well?

9. Eve told Sheila, "God can bring light into darkness." Have you found that to be true in your own life? Explain.

10. Why is the quilt important to Meredith? What significance does it have for Eve? Do you have an important memento from your childhood that you never could give away? Explain.

11. Eve wants her daughter to be tested for VHL. Why does Meredith hesitate to have the test done? If you learned you might have inher-

ited a debilitating or fatal medical condition, would you choose to be tested? Why or why not?

12. If Pete or Sheila asked you why God allows suffering, what would your answer be?

When her neighbor proposes a "practical" marriage, romantic Rene Mitchell throws the ring in his face. Fleeing Texas for Montana, Rene rides with trucker Clay Preston—and rescues an expectant mother stranded in a snowstorm. Clay doesn't believe in romance, but can Rene change his mind?

Turn the page for a sneak preview of
"A Dry Creek Wedding"
by Janet Tronstad,
one of the heartwarming stories about wedded
bliss in the new collection
SMALL-TOWN BRIDES.
Available in June 2009 from Love Inspired®.

"Never let your man go off by himself in a snow storm," Mandy said. The inside of the truck's cab was dark except for a small light on the ceiling. "I should have stopped my Davy."

"I doubt you could have," Rene said as she opened her left arm to hug the young woman. "Not if he thought you needed help. Here, put your head on me. You may as well stretch out as much as you can until Clay gets back."

Mandy put her head on Rene's shoulder. "He's going to marry you some day, you know."

"Who?" Rene adjusted the blankets as Mandy stretched out her legs.

"A rodeo man would make a good husband," Mandy muttered as she turned slightly and arched her back.

"Clay? He doesn't even believe in love."

Well, that got Mandy's attention, Rene thought,

as the younger woman looked up at her and frowned. "Really?"

Rene nodded.

"Well, you have to have love," Mandy said firmly. "Even my Davy says he loves me. It's important."

"I know." Rene wondered how her life had ever gotten so turned around. A few days ago she thought Trace was her destiny and now she was kissing a man who would rather order up a wife from some catalogue than actually fall in love. She'd felt the kiss he'd given her more deeply than she should, too. Which meant she needed to get back on track.

"I'm going to make a list," Rene said. "Of all the things I need in a husband. That's how I'll know when I find the right one."

Mandy drew in her breath. "I can help. For you, not for me. I want my Davy."

Rene looked out the side window and saw that the light was coming back to the truck. She motioned for Mandy to sit up again. She doubted Clay had found Mandy's boyfriend. She'd have to keep the young woman distracted for a little bit longer.

Clay took his hat off before he opened the door to his truck. Then he brushed his coat before climbing inside. He didn't want to scatter snow all over the women.

"Did you see him?" Mandy asked quietly from the middle of the seat.

Clay shook his head. "I'll need to come back."

"But—" Mandy protested until another pain caught her and she drew in her breath.

"It won't take long to get you to Dry Creek," Clay said as he started his truck. "Then I can come back and look some more."

Clay didn't like leaving the man out there any more than Mandy did, but it could take hours to find him, and the sooner they got Mandy comfortable and relaxed, the sooner those labor pains of hers would go away.

"I feel a lot better," Mandy said. "If you'd just go back and look some more, I'll be fine."

Clay looked at the young woman as she bit her bottom lip. Mandy was in obvious pain regardless of what she said. "You're not fine, and there's no use pretending."

Mandy gasped, half in indignation this time.

Those pains worried him, but he assumed she must know the difference between the ones she was having and ones that signaled the baby was coming. Women went to class for that kind of thing these days. She probably just needed to lie down somewhere and put her feet up.

"He's right," Rene said as she put her hand on

Mandy's stomach. "Davy wouldn't want you out here. He'll tell you that when we find him. And think of the baby."

Mandy turned to look at Rene and then looked back at Clay.

"You promise you'll come back?" Mandy asked. "Right away?"

"You have my word," Clay said as he started to back up the truck.

"That should be on your list," Mandy said as she looked up at Rene. "Number one—he needs to keep his word."

Clay wondered if the two women were still talking about the baby Mandy was having. It seemed a bit premature to worry about the little guy's character, but he was glad to see that the young woman had something to occupy her mind. Maybe she had plans for her baby to grow up to be president or something.

"I don't know," Rene muttered. "We can talk about it later."

"We've got some time," Clay said. "It'll take us fifteen minutes at least to get to Dry Creek. You may as well make your list."

Mandy shifted on the seat again. "So, you think trust is important in a husband?"

"A *husband?*" Clay almost missed the turn. "You're making a list for a husband?"

"Well, not for me," Mandy said patiently. "It's Rene's list, of course."

Clay grunted. Of course.

"He should be handsome, too," Mandy added as she stretched. "But maybe not smooth, if you know what I mean. Rugged, like a man, but nice."

Clay could feel Mandy's eyes on him.

"I don't really think I need a list," Rene said so low Clay could barely hear her.

Clay didn't know why he was so annoyed that Rene was making a list. "Just don't put Trace's name on that thing."

"I'm not going to put anyone's name on it," Rene said as she sat up straighter. "And you're the one who doesn't think people should just fall in love. I'd think you would *like* a list."

Clay had to admit she had a point. He should be in favor of a list like that; it eliminated feelings. It must be all this stress that was making him short-tempered. "If you're going to have a list, you may as well make the guy rich."

That should show he was able to join into the spirit of the thing.

"There's no need to ridicule—" Rene began.

"A good job does help," Mandy interrupted solemnly. "Especially when you start having babies.

I'm hoping the job in Idaho pays well. We need a lot of things to set up our home."

"You should make a list of what you need for your house," Clay said encouragingly. Maybe the women would talk about clocks and chairs instead of husbands. He'd seen enough of life to know there were no fairy tale endings. Not in his life.

* * * * *

Will spirited Rene Mitchell change trucker
Clay Preston's mind about love?
Find out in
SMALL-TOWN BRIDES,
the heartwarming anthology from
beloved authors Janet Tronstad
and Debra Clopton.
Available in June 2009 from Love Inspired®

REQUEST YOUR FREE BOOKS!
2 FREE RIVETING INSPIRATIONAL NOVELS
PLUS 2 FREE MYSTERY GIFTS

YES! Please send me 2 FREE Love Inspired® Suspense novels and my 2 FREE mystery gifts (gifts are worth about $10). After receiving them, if I don't wish to receive any more books, I can return the shipping statement marked "cancel." If I don't cancel, I will receive 4 brand-new novels every month and be billed just $4.24 per book in the U.S. or $4.74 per book in Canada, plus 25¢ shipping and handling per book and applicable taxes, if any*. That's a savings of over 20% off the cover price! I understand that accepting the 2 free books and gifts places me under no obligation to buy anything. I can always return a shipment and cancel at any time. Even if I never buy another book, the two free books and gifts are mine to keep forever.   123 IDN ERXX   323 IDN ERXM

Name	(PLEASE PRINT)	
Address		Apt. #
City	State/Prov.	Zip/Postal Code

Signature (if under 18, a parent or guardian must sign)

Order online at www.LoveInspiredSuspense.com
Or mail to Steeple Hill Reader Service:

IN U.S.A.: P.O. Box 1867, Buffalo, NY 14240-1867
IN CANADA: P.O. Box 609, Fort Erie, Ontario L2A 5X3

Not valid to current subscribers of Love Inspired Suspense books.

Want to try two free books from another series?
Call 1-800-873-8635 or visit www.morefreebooks.com

* Terms and prices subject to change without notice. N.Y. residents add applicable sales tax. Canadian residents will be charged applicable provincial taxes and GST. Offer not valid in Quebec. This offer is limited to one order per household. All orders subject to approval. Credit or debit balances in a customer's account(s) may be offset by any other outstanding balance owed by or to the customer. Please allow 4 to 6 weeks for delivery. Offer available while quantities last.

Your Privacy: Steeple Hill Books is committed to protecting your privacy. Our Privacy Policy is available online at www.SteepleHill.com or upon request from the Reader Service. From time to time we make our lists of customers available to reputable third parties who have a product or service of interest to you. If you would prefer we not share your name and address, please check here. ☐

LISUS08R

Love Inspired
SUSPENSE

TITLES AVAILABLE NEXT MONTH

On sale June 9, 2009

NO ALIBI by Valerie Hansen

Jury duty was just another chore for Julie Ann Jones—until the life at stake became her own. A series of "accidents" target the jurors, and while fellow juror Smith Burnett gives Julie Ann the courage to carry on, both Julie Ann and Smith may pay the ultimate price for justice.

HER LAST CHANCE by Terri Reed
Without a Trace

Missing mother—and suspected murderer—Leah Farley is found, but with no recollection of her past. If she can't reclaim her memories, even bounty hunter Roman Black won't be able to protect her from the *real* killer, who wants to keep Leah's lost secrets buried forever.

SCENT OF MURDER by Virginia Smith

Caitlin Saylor is dazzled when she meets Chase Hollister. The candle factory owner is handsome, charming and very interested in Caitlin. But when a special gift leaves Caitlin in danger, protecting her could cost Chase his business, his reputation—or maybe his life.

BLACKMAIL by Robin Caroll

When oil rigs are sabotaged, PR representative Sadie Thompson is put on the case. Then someone threatens Sadie and Caleb, her half-brother, to make the evidence disappear. Caleb's parole officer, Jon Garrison, is watching them both closely, waiting for one of them to slip up. He doesn't trust Sadie—can she trust him? She needs Jon's help, and has nowhere else to turn.